The Gizmo

by

Tito Perdue

Books by Tito Perdue

Lee (1991)
The New Austerities (1994)
Opportunities in Alabama Agriculture (1994)
The Sweet-Scented Manuscript (2004)
Fields of Asphodel (2007)
The Node (2011)
Morning Crafts (2013)
Reuben (2014)
The Builder: William's House I (2016)
The Churl: William's House II (2016)
The Engineer: William's House III (2016)
The Bachelor: William's House IV (2016)
Cynosura (2017)
Philip (2017)
Though We Be Dead, Yet Our Day Will Come
(2018)
The Bent Pyramid (2018)
The Philatelist (2018)
The Smut Book (2018)

The Gizmo

by

Tito Perdue

Standard American Publishing Company-
Brent, Alabama
2020

CONTENTS

For Tweedy

One

We are four people born on different dates who continue to be alive today. And if it's true that we gave too much time to study and reading, you ought at least credit us for enduring the miseries consequent upon too much knowledge too hastily acquired. In my own case, I will say that I never took advantage of my advantages, never sought to turn intelligence into money, never acceded to received opinion. On the contrary!

He grew up—(I am speaking of myself here)—in a small town where he did all those things that need to be done by young boys growing up in good times—hiking and fishing and stamp collecting. He followed girls, he had dogs, he attended birthday parties. He has built tree houses in his time, having stolen the lumber that the jobs required. Switching back to the first person singular, I had a rifle, and within ten minutes of home could set foot upon a thousand-acre field patrolled by crows. Or, I might keep vigil on winter nights from my dark roost on top the house. Indeed I did all manner of things, ending up on at least three occasions at the police station. And since you ask, yes I have kissed girls, some of them more than once. But even then, even as early at that, I had begun to experience the call of wisdom and information and their connected joys.

By age of sixteen I had been offered five several scholarships to schools both inside and outside the state. In the beginning I actually did attend (briefly) an elite academy in the nearest big city, but then shortly transferred over to a university that was larger than the town that sustained it. Intimidated at first by the girls and boys, by the professors and everything else, I remained mostly silent for about four months, which is to say until I had apprised myself of the quality and quiddities of my fellow students. Thereafter I never viewed myself as superior to anyone,

save only that great majority who opt to be inferior.
Passed thus a full year, until I was allowed to take a private room in the village, some two hundred and seventeen
paces from the library.

The library: I have always preferred thick books with
blue covers, especially old ones, and even more especially
if the pages have been inscribed with handwritten notes in
the margins. Never was I to forget an expertly drawn sail-
ing ship left behind on page 418 of a certain fat volume
that looked as if it had been soaking for hundreds of years
in salt water brine. Not that I was hostile to mint-new
books offering up-to-date information on a whole variety
of things. Of these, the best were slim volumes in lemon-
colored wrappers. I used to linger among my preferred
sections of the Dewey Decimal System and go through
these books one by one, paying more attention to the type
and illustrations than to the actual matter.

I still remained mostly silent most of the time. In
chemistry, I was expected to have a partner, but managed
to argue my way out of that. I never understood, then or
now, why people had rather come together and smile into
one another's face over cocktails than to work quietly behind locked doors in well-equipped laboratories. "If people knew what was good, they would do it," said the philosopher. Because good action, I think he meant to say,
redounds to the happiness of the person doing it. Accordingly I became more self-sufficient than ever, avoiding
more and more people every day and scoring better and
better grades, and gaining at last the key—there were but
six of these—to the rare books room. And if my health
suffered slightly, only very slightly really, it was the best
trade of my career.

Now when I turned eighteen, my philosophy instruc-
tor, a specialist in seventeenth-century necromancy, in-
troduced me to a middle aged "therapist," he called her, a
comely woman practiced in the arts that I had so far ne-

glected. I was never to know who paid for this, whether it was a jest, or gift, or a joint project by the members of the department. In any case it was largely because of this, I'm sure, that I was able to go about with a much more calm and focused attention than my . . . "peers," as I had almost started to call them.

You will want to know that in spite of its setting, I chose MIT for my graduate degrees. Torn between hard and soft sciences, between metaphysics and physics itself, I actually ended up in cell biology, a boring territory that however made available some sporadically interesting Federally-financed experimentation. Never since mowing lawns had I done a single day of nonintellectual work, and yet by the age of nineteen I had a three-room apartment full of books and furniture and some of the most up-to-date electronic devices. Had a car but lacked a dog. Ends here the prologue to my life and achievements.

Two

Spent three years in Brazil and had a romance with a Portuguese-speaking girl. You must allow that at that early date I still believed in the intellectual possibilities of women. It lasted until July, our little affair, whereupon I made her a gift of money and accompanied her to the station. The exchange rate then was highly favorable for those salaried in dollars, and I was able to pay stable charges for a palomino mare capable of carrying me up into the mountains and willing to stand by patiently as I fished the bright clear streams of that region. I learned the language, too. Or Portuguese I should have said, and not the strange mutterings of docile mares, who rarely spoke in any case.

My responsibilities had to do with molecules. It was believed, correctly, that the Brazilian flora had given discrete expression to all sorts of compounds applicable to medicine and industry and national aggression. My job therefore was to isolate these promising structures, take them apart, and put them back together again (even against their will if necessary) in altered form. We already knew there was no theoretical limit to size, but smallness, too, we proved, continues on to infinity and beyond. You take your garden-variety proton and break it all apart, you'll find that sucker's got all sorts of stuff in it. Three years of this and I had come up with two (2) structures never seen before, or not by earthlings anyway.

I was wasting my life. It is the responsibility of the superior person to *supersede* himself, and in that endeavor, I had made hardly any progress at all. And then, too, I was sick unto death with the debased culture of Latin America, the songs and dances, the puppet shows and yo-yo experts, the transactions going on in alleys, the country's human substrate, the military people, the women, the steel and glass buildings imitated from New York.

Is it possible that humans have no value? As compared to the Andromeda Galaxy for example? Either life offers supernal values, or else nothing matters, a lesson taught to me by South America.

I left Brazil with $42,550 in cash money, $327 in race track winnings, and just over $19,000 from my redeemable retirement account. Retirement? How I yearned for exactly that. It's also true that I had accrued a reasonable wardrobe (nine good suits and any number of hand-painted ties) that had to be forwarded to my hometown in northwestern Oklahoma. The mare I left behind.

And then I dallied. Glad to reacquaint myself with the northern sky, I took apart the family's disused barn and used the lumber for a diminutive laboratory measuring not much more than fourteen feet in width and about twenty long. Here, supplied with electricity, water, propane, and a deal of glassware, I carried out projects intended more for the amusement of the neighboring children than for the progress of science. And then, too, I had my old bedroom once again, the bedstead my grandfather had built, and the colored quilts composed by the woman who had given birth to the woman who had given birth to me. For my walls I had a copy of one of Jawlensky's early works and a historical engraving commemorating Jackson's victory at New Orleans. I had a window that looked out over a hundred and twenty-acre field that my people once had owned. The land was ours no more, but I still liked to wake at dawn and amble on down to the Pefley River, so-called, along with my fishing equipment and the family dog.

Of brothers, I once had two. It was in order to halt the expansion of a certain doctrine that was anyway fated to collapse a few years later that the government disposed of my best brother in a place in southeast Asia. The other boy, older than me, was subsumed into the scum of 1968 and slaughtered himself with cocaine, or heroin, or something of that kind. Sisters I had none.

In California, the gold fields were mostly exhausted by now, and so instead I went to Philadelphia where opportunities for people of my temperament proved to be extraordinarily thin. And besides, I wanted an intermission for getting back into my books—Evola, Spengler, Sunić, Kurtagić, and others brought to my notice by good-intentioned angels.

It hardly needs saying that I soon became exasperated with the commotion, the television and newspapers, the flat-top buildings shaped like dominoes set on end. Especially I wearied of being robbed in broad daylight by street negroes with knives and other implements. And so by August I found myself in New York (the city) with its even taller negroes and even more glass buildings. Except that here the windows were generally covered with quicksilver, and whereas the brokers and bookies and consultants and PR people could see *out*, we others could not see *in*.

It was (is) the worst place in the world. I used to buy a
soft drink and sandwich and sit upon the curb to marvel
at the people passing in review. Two weeks of this and I
was able to construct a classification system for the human varieties to be seen, men in suits and women in
pricey shoes. At some point in history it had been en-
joined on people that their clothes have no stains on
them. Why? But mostly it were the males, and that wom-
en, the less unattractive members of the species, were
sometimes willing to connect with these things. Like pil-
grims they moved forward hypnotically, their eyes fixed
upon their downtown work places where money could be
had. But could they gut a hog, or build a fire without materials, or go a week without a waxing? My contempt increased.

There *were* some pretty good bookshops in that city—I
admit that—and some of the whores were damnably
good-looking. I used to stare at them, making their outer
layers invisible by dint of scientific knowledge until
naught was left of those people but a caul of pus and gore.
They didn't like that. Turned inside out, the women
looked like . . . He couldn't say exactly what. One had to
laugh, thinking of the desire invested in those organisms
by ignorant men.

Those were the days when I would read both deeply
and wide while gazing down upon a blistered landscape of
rooftops with dead pigeons on them. The sidewalks gave
off heat waves, and the cars, made of glossy metal instead
of varnished cherry, the cars, as I was saying, were so
much less aesthetical than ordinary mediaeval hay wains
that I turned away forever from all things not made either
of rock, peat, paper, cedar, soapstone, and a few other materials. Really, have ever there been more painterly dwell-
ings than turfen cottages with goats grazing on the roof?

I sought and unfortunately was granted a position with
a pharmaceutical company. (No, nothing had ever been

better than turfen cottages of that sort.) Never will I forget the credo of that organization, namely that good medicine is profitable medicine, and the other way around. The place was staffed by golf players and feminists with PhDs. I made no friends until my third year, when I was confronted by a master chemist and part-time mystic committed to an obscure branch of Sri Lankan Buddhism. The man remained in place for almost five months before being "let go" on account of incompatibility, hygiene, ethnocentrism, and other violations of his contractual penumbras and emanations. Me, I had actually read my contract in advance. Even so, I would have been let go, too, but for those patented molecules I carried everywhere I went.

I could do without friends, not without music. Even in New York, good music was sometimes on offer, and I used to leave my two-room apartment in one of Brooklyn's more vibrant, indeed pungent districts and take the train, the subway, the bus, and then walk the remaining half-mile to a certain famous concert hall where I could be confident of a more or less refined-looking crowd standing quietly in line for tickets, or to use the restroom at intermission. But when Wagner was playing, that was when I went entirely for the music and not for anything else.

It was here I almost made a friend. Seated next to each other beneath the grand chandelier, we shared the man's printed program that the usher had failed to provide me. This led to comments, and comments to agreement, and this in turn inspired the other man to turn away each time he coughed, an unprecedented piece of courtesy on the part of a New Yorker.

"It is popularly believed," he told me, "that beauty is for the benefit of humanity, the precise reverse of the real situation."

"How do you mean?" I asked innocently.

"Well! Beauty isn't enslaved to us, but us to beauty."

Unfortunately my friend seemed to experience a heart

attack or something of that nature before the performance was over, a disruption that caused him to stand and go away and never come back anymore.

Three

No one has asked for this. Even so, I want to get it down on paper for the good of the psychologists of the future. Also for my descendants, if only I had been provided any. Truth was, I was weary of just about everything, of breathing and sleeping and most of all of *thinking*, an unstoppable compulsion that kept people at a distance and sometimes had me calling out in the streets of the city. Books, too, began to pall on me, unless of course they were old and in yellow covers, bore fingerprints and obscure glosses, and had been consigned to that special room in the library where the best stuff was held at constant temperature and humidity. We understood each other, me and those who had troubled to make comments, usually in Latin, in the margins of old books. Not that I could very easily decipher that handsome-looking language.

At that period, anyone seeing me close up or even at a distance would have classed me as more or less a normal person. My height was respectable, and though my face had become largely indeterminate, my courtesy was a delight to any who came within range of it. I required paisley for my ties while my cufflinks, with one exception, all bore Grecian themes. As to my head and its contents, these were as clear and as brilliant in my youth as when I was to find myself at age seventy-six on Death's agenda. Having no need for wealth, my wealth went on growing. And if at one time I had hankered for someone to talk to, I was soon to be given three persons of that sort exactly.

Because in January that year, he (me) learned something new and fateful about isotopic bismuth and antigravity rays, something to do with one of my molecules. This in turn brought me those acquaintanceships that I no longer sought, to wit three other persons very like myself in age, irritability, genius, and astigmatic condition. We used to meet in the afterhours on Thursdays, and in company with various kinds of liquors and other treats, talk about a whole raft of things. Seven months of this and we had learned how to deal with quantum bonding in the same way as bees with Texas bluebonnets in the month of May.

My new friends! Beginning from the bottom, there was a seventy-three-year-old physicist from Oregon known pseudonymously as "Casper Grey." His brains were just fine, and his comments always to the point. For such an educated and reasonable-looking person, his wife was the most awful human being since MIT. Truth was, she had taken part in the feminist convulsion and had consequently become so much like a man that her husband had felt constrained to do what had to be done. (More about this later on.) I liked him a good deal, though not quite so much as for example K------------, who stood closer to my own age. The best theorist of us all, he used to draw equations in the palm of his hand, sometimes continuing over to his forearm and even unto the elbow on special occasions. He lived on medicines, and his nose was so swollen that a close examination exposed minute crustaceans harboring in his pores. Like me, he took joy in the misfortunes of others, and like me yearned for life to come to an end. A handsome man in his youth, he had caused numbers of women to fall in love with him, plain ordinary girls whom he always abandoned at the last moment, a greater pleasure, he claimed, than ordinary sex.

And then there was Earl ("Earl the Pearl"), next to me the best of the whole bunch. Him I really did appreciate, both for his acquirements and the cozy apartment and well-structured wife he maintained in the 4000 block of

16th Avenue in Manhattan. We used to draw off into his library and wait there quietly until the wonderful woman who was his wife had brought out the pastries and warm fudges that drew us to this place. Her figure, both above and below the waist, was good to look at, and in short she seemed to have come to us direct from the 1950s. Somewhat belatedly, I realized that Casper had been speaking:

"The things that we could do!" he said, referring to the device we had put together with positron extruders and little bits and pieces of leftover software confiscated from "Greenwillow Laboratories," as the government had named the place. "And turn that Gehenna" (contemporary civilization) "upside down!"

"Easy," I cautioned. "Slow down. We need to think about this. We don't have to destroy *everything* just to make *some* things better."

"True," said K. "And besides, some things really are very nice even as they stand. This here fudge for example, to name just one."

"One? You've had six pieces already!"

"Yes, yes, we know you're good at counting."

"Let's take it out and look at it, you want to? The gizmo I mean?"

We waited in seeming calmness as Earl went to the cabinet, opened the second drawer from the bottom, gently lifted out the "gizmo," we called it, and set it tenderly in the middle of the table. At that date no one could have guessed the notoriety that would accrue to this device, or that by the early 2020s, marketed under the trade name of "escrubilator," it was destined to replace computers and DIY transgendering kits in terms of sales. Slowly we four moved in a circle around the table, gazing adoringly on our creation.

"Just look at that son-of-a bitch! You want to know what genius looks like? Just look at this."

"We need to build some sort of housing for it. So no

one can know what it is."

"They wouldn't know what it is if we shoved it up their noses. But yes, we really ought to have something to put it in."

We moved closer. Not much larger than a shoebox, the instrument allowed it to be seen what it was composed of, namely a confusion of coils and tubes and a concave bar of bismuth in a state of high excitation. It possessed all sorts of competencies, our invention, but none more impressive than the ability to disaggregate a human individual from 20 miles distance by fixing on that person's facial identity. Even a photograph sufficed.

"There's the business right there," said K, touching the thing with his index finger. He had no obvious fear of it, knowing as he did that it hadn't been activated as yet. He was a large man with a large nose.

"Masters of the world! Gives one a strange feeling, no?"

"Yes it does. But I can't say it's particularly unpleasant, that feeling you're talking of."

We smiled and gloated and toasted each other with 40 mm beakers of rosé wine. Having studied the thing for about a minute and a half, Earl now lifted it gingerly, transported it back to the cabinet, and wrapped it up in swaddling clothes.

Four

Four days later I invested in a performance of the *Götterdämmerung*, not knowing that it was to be presented in modern dress. Unwilling to ask for a refund from the snotty-looking ticket seller sitting athwart her stool with a peace symbol dangling from her neck, I exited the theatre with indignation and ventured out into the doomed city that lay all about in every direction. Really, could aught be more disquieting than a post-modern conurbation with a demographic as abnormal as New York City's? Hadn't gone half a block before I encountered a tall thin queer in black lipstick wearing the tattoo of a hat on his shaven head. I stepped past a beggar with an accordion, and then, moving against the current at the bottom of the "sea," as this district always appeared to me, I found myself in danger of the outlandish specimens that came up to meet me, squids and octopi with hundreds of eyes. I stopped in front of an all-night gymnasium full of youngish people carrying out clownish actions with weights and pulleys, narcissists in iridescent uniforms. Impossible not to laugh. Fifty years had gone by since I had last given credence to the actions of ordinary people. What did they want, these types? Came then a restaurant full of diners munching energetically just on the other side of the window, a distance of perhaps just 20 inches from where I stood. Gazing into the faces of those human mockups, I had suddenly to reach out and brace myself against one of the innumerable signposts, mailboxes, pedestrians, or telephone poles that punctuated the city. Is this what life is for? A pullulating fauna with needs and itches? Tubes of shit acuminating in smiling faces? A sexualized species testing the air for one another's crotches? Miles of intestines for turning inoffensive creatures into shit? And was it really better on other planets? And if not, why should people like my friends and me go on living?

As proof of courage, I had proposed to walk all the way to Queens and back, which is to say until I remembered how far it was. Instead I strode to the next nearest restaurant and after making a hurried survey of the clientele, entered by way of a rotating pentagonal glass door in which an elderly woman had become ensnared. I wanted a table whence I could spy upon the outside pedestrians, which seemed entirely fair to me insofar as I had so recently been a pedestrian, too. Instead, the hostess, a near relative of the aforementioned ticket vendor, ushered me to the last place I wanted, never ask me where.

Considered as a group the men, all wearing non-coordinated suits and earrings, seemed quite well-fed enough already. Men's fashions now required their garments to be out of chime with each other, such that it was not unusual to see hostile hues all mixed up together. (It marked the beginning of mismatched shoes.) One man, an actor or artist or revolutionary was dressed in sandals and had a long grey beard. How was it possible, that these prosperous and sophisticated citizens of the World City should be gullible enough for this, for childish disguises and such long grey beards? Just then my thinking leaped forward a couple of thousand years, granting me the prospect of a new Daphnis and future Chloe frolicking in green rolling hills where New York City used to be.

I wanted to slaughter the whole mass of them and send their residues into outer space. What, really, did they want? Whatever it was, they wanted it greatly. I saw two ambigendered couples at the next table, all four of them speaking simultaneously. As for the women, their teeth were white, their noses powdered, and their skirts so short that the florescent lighting had driven large black spiders from their orifices. The men were worse, office building thralls wasting away their lives on paperwork. Was this better than slaughtering Persians, or harvesting figs in Boeotia? The answer was "certainly not," and after I had consumed my pre-prandial daiquiri I, tried to turn my thoughts to nobler things.

By 11:46 I had arrived back at my apartment (which I haven't described as yet), and then constructed for myself a rather better daiquiri than the one that had cost me $27.00 plus city, state, and diversity taxes. My dwelling was a suite of two large rooms and one wee one, all of them painted a dark emerald green and all full of such massy furniture as that hardly enough room was left over for a person to blunder from place to place in search of books and drink. The carpeting was poor. On the other

hand, the floor was built of heavy oaken planks in which
the termites had made only the most inconsequential
progress before giving up on it and going away. I had
money, and this is how I had elected to use it, for dark
heavy furniture, for weaponry, for an ultraviolet telescope,
and for advanced television equipment that let me pick up
the video transmissions of a famous rocket ship now in its
22nd year of travel. Taking up position on my leather sofa,
I many a time fell off to sleep under the influence of stars
and quartzitic landscapes merging in and out of view.

No need to list my books, save to mention that there
were a great many of them and that they also served as a
kind of insulation both against cold weather and voices
from other rooms. In fact my neighbors on both sides
were predominantly silent, and only in the beginning had
any of them actually tried to greet me in the hall or lobby
or the elevator with its very limited weight load capacity.
In addition, my landlady was a discrete person, or else was
afraid of me, and so seldom spoke in my presence that I
could scarce remember which face was hers. All my bills
were paid on time and in the case of rent, given six
months in advance.

Returning to books, I had given up on fiction when female writers began to be promoted. Good at mnemonic
work only, they had ventured into matters far beyond
their range. On the other hand, I did read more philosophy than ever before, reveling in Evola and Spengler, Pefley and Guénon, in Nietzsche of course, not to forget Kurtagić and Yockey and a dozen other bright and brilliant
men able to diagnose our current disgrace. Culture, not
economics, is the substrate of society, and cultures are
prone to disease.

For routine company (not that I needed any), I had
imported three (3) *Jackson's Chameleons*, my favorite of
the reptiles. With non-coördinated eye beams, these creatures are able to assimilate twice the information in half

the time, becoming four times wiser four times faster. Contained in an enormous custom-built glass aquarium tank ($2,032), I had tried to give my little pets the territory, the victuals, and entertainments they required. I used to take them out and tease them from time to time, especially when I had a beverage nearby and had homed in on the transmissions of the *Reverend Martin Luther King, Jr.*, as the space ship was named.

I never got bored. Let's admit it, that when a person is blessed with a certain sort of mind, a "beehive," as it were, filled with thoughts and loathing, ennui is quite impossible. I used to stand at the window and look down with fascination into the most fissiparous and reductionistic society ever seen. Because decadence, I had learnt, is more awful than cannibalism. Suddenly that moment my television was interrupted by an emergency broadcast reporting that durables were up but comestibles were down. A loud groan could be heard from the apartment next door. Came next a talk show host adored worldwide for her sexual abnormalities.

I remain proud of my small (but expensive) hoard of pharmaceuticals, especially those designed to hold off total despair. Innocent-looking little pills, pale pink in color and shaped like various animals, I normally take one each morning and, in order to ward off nightmares, three at night. Out of the body experiences? I could only hope so. No, this corpse of mine, all 202 pounds of it, continued to cleave parasitically to me like an avocado to its seed. It had to be fed, etc. I had to buy clothes for it. And yet my case was significantly happier than that of my friend Casper Grey, a remarkable sort of person first brought to your attention a few pages above.

Five

An ordinary genius of the intuitive kind, he (Casper) at

the time of this report was just slightly older than Earl. As
to how he had managed to survive to that age must be left
to future investigators. Admittedly, it does sometimes
happen in even the most benighted periods that a good
person will be able to hold "his head above the surface of
the slurry," and prove himself not just a genius but a hero
as well.

Born in the prelapsarian South, he had served bravely
in one of the country's early campaigns against small,
weak, and victorious countries. Having left behind the
lower three-quarters of his right leg, he had used the government's compensation money to enter a much-lauded
northeastern university where he remained just ten days.
Not that they were sorry to see him go, him with his open,
frank, and unpretentious ways. Returning to Tennessee on
one leg (more about this a little further on), he then entered a small, unranked private college patronized mostly
by local boys destined for careers in diesel repair, drafts-
manship, air conditioning, and the like. Here he thrived,
or at least until the Federals uncovered the racial make-up
of the school and contrived to shut it down.

Followed then two years in silence, until his money ran
out. Later on, looking back upon that period, he would
mention his one-room suite, the unsound bed, his kidney-
shaped desk, and the estimated 319 books he had sucked
dry while lying out in the yard, or in the front porch
swing. As for food and other things, he seems to have had
very little of either. And nothing at all of girls. And in
brief, this was how he became, as he said, "the world's
most knowledgeable human being. With perhaps one or
two others notwithstanding," he sometimes admitted.

Eventually he needed funds, and by age of twenty-eight
had proved so valuable to a state laboratory responsible
for the quality control of highway materials that he was
allowed to come and go pretty much as he pleased. Here
among some hundred state government employees—he

liked them—he was able to take long walks in the countryside, attend lectures, and sate himself on books, music,
and dreams. He might come to work and stay for just an
hour or two. Or disappear for three days at a time. "I never
saw the dignity of it," he said. "Grownup men and women
spinning out their lives to the dictates of the clock. How'd
this fashion get started in the first place? Strewth!"

At last, with several thousand dollars of money to his
account, he traveled to New York City where right away
he was arrested for having taken a beating from three vibrant persons. Forgetting he had one leg only, he had actually tried to *kick* one of his victims, ending up on the
sidewalk in the 300 block of Long Street, a busy thorough-
fare named after a Civil War personality. It was here he
had lost his eye, his wallet, and his vest pocket notebook
holding two expired lottery tickets and the name, address,
and schematics of a girl in it.

Life went on, and in August he married an educated
and not unhandsome woman who in the fullness of time
joined the feminist movement. Year by year he watched as
day by day she turned into a careerist, a bitch, and at last a
man. *Four years* he endured, right up until the woman
"disappeared," it was reported. I've already said he was a
hero, and when the woman's philosophy was uncovered
and brought forward, the authorities dropped the case. I
also said he was a genius, a chemist, an autodidact, and
was proficient in causing things to "disappear" as it were.
Or as it wasn't, to bring a bit of mirth to bear.

By now his self-sufficiency was almost complete. Able
to appease his sexual requirements with an implement he
had devised, he turned forever away from women and
thereafter followed the laws so literally that the D.A. finally lost all interest in him. Like Howard (my very self) he
dressed like a perfectionist and was able to get bank loans
he hadn't the least intention of acquitting. From Germany
he had bought at high cost an ingenious piece of equip-

ment, a sort of "proto-escrubilator" (to speak of it that way), capable of replicating currencies, license plates, passports, tax receipts, search warrants, court judgments, diplomas, military citations, police reports, and the like. He relocated every half-year at the minimum, staying usually in Montevideo or Klagenfurt. Full of money and knowledge, he had put aside all the usual recreations and by age of seventy-three had begun to turn his attention to the most serious and most portentous question of all, namely this post-modern age and what to do about it. This then was the man and these his resources when first I came to know him.

Not very long before, I had contributed to a *Festschrift* in honor of a philologist (now dead), whom I once admired. Finding a place among the shelves of the Klagenfurt library, this rather perfunctory essay of mine had been seen by Casper, in consequence of which I was handed a six-page letter arriving at my apartment in late April of that year. Here now was a man I could talk to, a splenetic person, educated and logical, someone ready to retaliate upon the world before he grew too old for action. Of course I replied, never mentioning my own scheme until the closing paragraph of that incautious letter. Followed then three weeks of silence, in turn followed by the man himself tapping, tapping as of someone rapping, rapping at my chamber door.

He was tall and thin, and presented an appearance of one of my least favorite types. His replacement eye had been wrongly mounted, causing the thing forever to be staring up dolefully at the sky. Too, his goiter reminded me of a certain old-time professor of mine, while as for the face in general, it was too dark and narrow and tended to bring the eyes, the good and the bad, into too great propinquity, one to another. No, it didn't just "tend" to do that. It *did*.

"Well!" said I. (I had been reorganizing the L–N section

in my bookcase and was dressed in an apron with an image of squirrels and flowers on it. I needed time to assimilate the man's appearance, his briefcase, and velveteen suit. His pockets were obviously very heavy-laden, putting his suspenders under conspicuous stress. I despised his tie, a blue one with the usual stripes on it. Better he had chosen one with squirrels and flowers.) "Well," said I, as I've said already. "Not from the IRS are you?"

He chuckled in an obligatory sort of way and then stepped past me, leaving me looking in an outdated direction.

"How was your flight?"

"Good, good. Quite good. Where's the . . . instrument?"

"I have it. We can look at it later. Have you breakfasted?"

"Is it, for example, real big and heavy? Like a dish washer for example? Or is it small and compact, say like the Antikythera Mechanism, or one of those fourth generation attitudinal recentering devices?"

"Larger than a dime, but smaller than a cow."

"Splendid! If I could, like, have anything l wanted, I do believe I'd ask to look at it now."

"Coffee first, no? And don't you want to freshen up?"

"Freshen up? My wife used to say that. If you're asking if I need to use the toilet, the answer is yes I do."

I conduced this rather strange individual to the facility where he immediately slammed shut the door and locked it several times. I had a television set in that room and soon I could hear the familiar voice of one of the blond-headed beauties who nowadays give the news. Concerning his briefcase, he had taken that with him. Based upon his peculiar ways, I admit that I had begun to dislike him a little bit less than before. Was this in truth the man who had read a thousand books in five different languages? Or were it the other way around?

We dined that night at my favorite delicatessen, a dark, noisy, and narrow establishment not much more than seventeen foot wide. The place was full of anti-American foods of all sorts—soft cheeses and sausages and pickled eggs in an oil of some kind. It were also full of bohemian types—we looked at each other—advanced people mooting about films and revolution. Revolution? If they could but know the *true* revolutionist in that establishment, the one in a five-hundred-dollar suit!

"Maybe we could see the device after supper," my associate speculated.

"That's entirely possible."

"Speaking of which, just look at that piece of shit sitting over there with the curdled expression on her face. Belongs to the richest segment of world history while suffering from the most extreme discontent."

"Victimized. She's been victimized."

"And that one!" (My friend had to rise from his chair to point him out.) The man had a piercing in his left eyelid and was too exhausted to sit up straight. One hand had five rings on it while the other was continually lifting up abnormal-looking shrimp and condemning them one by one to the ordeal of his unusual-looking teeth. An expensive operation, the opalization process had given his dentition a fascinating glow. I then descried a single drop of bright red wine or mayhap blood working its way ever so slowly to the point of his chin where inevitably it must someday lose its adhesion and fall into his rice. Old as I was, and am, I could easily have slain the boy with my carving knife.

"Even you Casper, heck I believe even you could do it."

"Make it a joint enterprise."

Meantime I was enjoying my crab cakes and ethical seaweed reconstituted to taste like asparagus. Regaling myself with generous swigs of black Czech beer, I could feel my loathing of modernity somewhat attenuating the more I drank. To preserve it (the loathing), I turned to watch a crowd of college students come to indulge the assumed bohemianism of the place. Really, would it be better to slay these, or the examples described above?

"Wish you had brought the escrubilator with you?"

"Maybe. Actually, I'm just not quite ready to use the thing as yet. I admit it."

"What did you say just now?"

"Not quite ready."

"Jeez, Howard! What's it's going to take? I mean! It's not as if you built that thing all by yourself."

"I understand that. We couldn't have done it without your formula."

"How long Howard, how long? Think you'll be ready when you're ninety? You could die on us! Any day now!"

"I understand that. Hell, I probably understand it even better than you."

"OK, give it to me, alright? I'll put it where it won't get hurt. And you can come and visit with it every day."

Six

I was sorry to have relinquished the thing, particularly after sitting through a newscast boasting the actions of front-line women combatants in hand-to-hand operations in Kirgizstan. Who was responsible for using women this way, and how many of such persons could be put to death with just one spurt from the apparatus that had so recently been in my keeping? That was when I stumbled upon a channel where some dozen jigaboos were dancing obscenely to the tribal music associated with that demographic. Black grinning faces interlarded with bumps and grinds. I wanted to vomit. Truly, these people had not measurably progressed since first brought into Pharaoh's astounded presence.

I passed over the following few channels, pausing brief-

ly at a comedy show where the jokes were weak, the
laughter enormous, and the subject matter mostly about
human elimination and body parts. I found a historical
show concerning the War of 1812 with fuck scenes interlarded between the battles. Came I then to a police drama
featuring a black man of great integrity and a svelte woman trained in advanced methods of self-defense. I alit upon a channel in which a team of black polo players were
being served cocktails by intimidated white males. Who
was responsible for this, and why this mania to derogate
the only modern race apt for science and government and
the quest for transcendence? Me, I always chose quality
over fairness, wherefore I desired a world that was entirely
white. The others? Allow them very kindly to rot, so far as
I could care.

I quickly reviewed two more channels, each worse than
all the others, and then turned back to where new areas of
the cosmos were being seen for the first time by members
of our species. Someday—I was sure of it—a far better genus would be found, people who had shucked off their
bodies and could read at light speed in their floating
apartment houses.

In the days that followed, K had a party. "With no bodies," he asked, "why should they want apartment houses?"
Far from floating, his own apartment was a wretched sort
of thing and still had his mother living in it. Having just
turned seventy-six, he was allowed to slice the cake and to
apportion each member just as much as that person in his
opinion deserved to have. He should have been senile by
now, reckoning by his age, his industrial injuries, his diseases, his time in New York City, and his "mother," he
called her, a middle age individual whom he had found
blundering down 4th Avenue all those years ago. Hope-
lessly addicted to something or another, she had allowed
herself to be interviewed where she had fallen and had

agreed enthusiastically to be taken back to K's foreclosed residence. The woman, said to have shown ethnocentric tendencies, had been innovatively interrogated some five years previously and had lost the ability to speak, an attractive feature in K's mind, who wanted someone to do housework in return for meals and a pallet of her own. No, he never touched her. She wasn't the least bit attractive and had to be reminded to take baths.

By error, a young (far too young) software kook had been invited to join us, a pleasant enough chap, though still several years short of septuagenarian rank. It didn't need any great amount of conversation before he realized that he was "out of his depth," insofar as age and spirituality were involved. Casper had promised to unveil the gizmo and let us gaze at last upon the housing that he had put together out of mahogany and monkey hide. We were nervous of course, all of us, and I perhaps most of all. Anyway it's time to admit that I had suffered from various emotional irregularities at different points in my career, a well-attested response to excess genius brought into focus at too early an age. People familiar with this condition will sympathize with my situation. Said K: There's not a person in this room Howard, who hasn't had the same experience."

"Of course."

We were served with coffee and *petit fours*, not to mention the rather ridiculous party hats supplied by K's "mother." Mine was yellow, had a bill, and came to a point. The pastries soon were gone, leaving us in silence until the woman had retired to her special place. K's own hat was tall and white, and resembled those that chefs are wont to wear.

"May we look at the . . . *item* now Casper? With your consent?"

"You may look at it any time you wish! It's not as if I had built the thing all by myself, for Pete's sakes."

"Now there's a true word. About ten percent, I would say. Ole Earl and me, we did the hard stuff."

"What!"

"Now I know how Bruno must have felt. Do the work and let others take the credit. No, I don't mind. Really."

"Oh, he minds alright. Look at him."

"Let a couple of security people come barging in here, and I'm going to let y'all have *all* the credit."

"Except that your fingerprints are all over that hickey. They'll put you in the electric chair." He grabbed up his party horn and pointing it in my direction, blasted at me.

"Good ole Howie, always trying to evade responsibility." (This man's hat was green and resembled the headwear of the vanished Phrygians.)

"I see. I was fetched here so you could deliver yourself of all the insults you've been hoarding up. No really K, you should see yourself in that hat."

Some laughed, some smiled, and some finished off their coffees and pushed the cups away. There was a considerable noise coming from upstairs where K's mother seemed to be auditing half a dozen television shows at the same time. Was this the sort of people to turn the world around? To slay, let us say, 10,000 bad people and return the country to more normal ways? To inculcate transcendent values and persuade the race to pay more attention to itself? Finally Casper said this:

"Alright, I'm fixing to take the gizmo out so we can look at it. But then we have to make some decisions, know what I mean?"

Earl raised his hand. "I do."

"Excellent. Tell us."

"Well, first we need to . . ."

"Stand up."

Earl stood. His hat was as blue as the paper used to make it. "Well, we need . . ."

"Swallowing your vowels again. Stand up straight man,

so we can hear you!"

"Remember, we're only four little monads seeking entelechy."

"Right. Well, first we need to decide who needs to be . . ."

"Discontinued."

"Right. Someone in government? Or someone in the arts?"

"Arts of course. That's the only thing that matters in the long run. And Hitler thought so, too."

"I might agree with that, if we had artists of any account. No, I vote for killing government people."

"Good! No, I feel like we're beginning to make real progress now. Any suggestions as to who?"

All four monads raised their hands. But at that point, and to prevent these people from impeaching themselves in open print, the chapter slowed and trundled forward for just another word or two.

Seven

Having already assigned Earl the honor of lifting out the gizmo, of holding it aloft and then of turning about slowly in a circle to afford everyone a view of the gold leaf inscription from Bacchylides, we gathered around and waited for the event. It is true that one of the members, never mind who, wasn't competent in Greek and required the help of another person, myself actually, who never asked for praise for this or any other endeavor. Don't need it, praise, and don't have any use for it. I now took the mechanism over into my own hands and cradled it ever so gently in the crook of my more reliable arm. If any man or group deserves to be sacrificed on behalf of history, surely this was the tool for doing it. By comparison, the national blade of France was a disgraceful thing, crude beyond measure, whileas for firearms and daggers and the like, we spit upon weapons of that kind. Either we kill with *genius*, or allocate the work to someone else.

We four had all the chemistry and physics we could have wanted, but it wasn't until Earl had been discovered and recruited and his loathing of decadence attested, it wasn't until then that we had our IT expert. Married to the last best woman in New York—(being last, she really couldn't fail to be best)—committed also to the quantum computer purchased by him at terrific cost, affiliated as he was with the Uruguayan Office of Police Statistics, a friend of the American Union of Attorneys General, intoxicated on knowledge and angry about his post-modern sons, it had proved easy to incorporate him into the group.

"Kill 'em all!" he was accustomed to saying. "Want to kill my son? Be my guest! The son-of-a-bitch hasn't the least interest in giving me heirs and yet continues to copulate almost every week!" And later:

"We had us a good country once. Pretty good anyway. Remember when children used to play outdoors all day long and come home tired? When people had front porches? When it were the boys who were nasty and girls were sweet? Why I used to be able to go downtown and see nothing but decent people."

"What do you see now Earl?"

"Fat men in short pants."

"Anybody else?" (We liked to urge him on.)

"Foreigners of course. More foreigners than people."

"But Earl, we *are* a nation of immigrants after all."

"A nation? We haven't been a nation since Eisenhower died. We used to be a nation with an economy; now we're just an economy with a bunch of foreigners chasing along behind. Like to kill ever last stinking one of 'em!"

"Whew. Tell us more about your sons."

"I haven't finished talking about foreigners yet!"

"Sorry."

"Did you know they're importing people from Africa

now? We don't have enough."

"Why are they doing this to us Earl? That's what people want to know."

"Why? Why? Because we've been so successful! Up to now, that is. Success is evil and must be punished. Remember how things used to be? When women were normal and the country was under the rule of its best people?"

"Tell us more about your children."

"Liberals and rich. One's in public relations and the other's a goddamn consultant!"

"Yikes."

"Farming, blacksmithing, wheelwrights, *those* are the real professions."

We laughed and then came forward one by one to stroke him on the head. We would give him his pin later on, a piece of iron about the size of a coin with the image on it of a rattlesnake rampant quartered with sword and ballpoint pen.

He was to prove a most valuable addition. The city had libraries, libraries in scads, all of them teeming over with the most interesting material. Earl, familiar with government publications, psephological studies, insurance claims, quarterly reports, postal receipts, patent applications, Micronesian school books, green savings stamps, gazetteers, telephone directories, and a mass of kindred information, had developed a list of the one-hundred-twenty-seven authorities most culpable of having enabled mass immigration. We were surprised by the names, and disappointed that as many as half of them had died already. We hesitated to ask Earl to research the addresses of their descendants, although as our newest member he was keen to take that project on as well.

He was to have undergone initiation on Wednesday, but instead came down just twenty-four hours earlier with a recurring gastric attack that put him to bed. It's not so terrible, a thing like that, not when a person has a wife like his. I could imagine the woman bending over him emolliently, her face saddened and her golden breasts dragging across his chest. And where pray were *my* wife and breasts? And why go on any longer in the absence of life's one only consolation?

Casper was out of town, and K was in therapy; accordingly I went downtown quite alone and wasted an hour at the corner of 5th and Alinsky, a vibrant and yeasty neighborhood with a great many substandard individuals in it. Here I stalled in front of a women's shop where some half-dozen manikins, unfeasibly slender, were wearing pastel dresses topped off with disquieting facial expressions. As customary with me I, too, was dressed with good taste, a precaution against the police. The crowd was silent and alert, though not so alert as on that day when a heaven-sent comet will have at last taken aim on the place. Enchanted by that possibility, I halted in the middle of the block, ignited a cigarette, and pushed my mind forward to the looting that would take place that promised day. I envisioned people running off with basketball shoes, recordings of bad music, gemstones, semi-automatics, and choice cuts of meat. And then as the comet comes nearer, thousands masturbating frantically in the streets and on top of buildings. That was when I experienced a policeman nudging me in the lower ribs with his black rubber wand. In my delirium, I had forgot that I was using a cigarette.

By 10:17 I had taken up a position on the southwest corner of the intersection and had begun reconnoitering the crowd. In my father's day, no one would have dreamt of going downtown in sandals without socks and underwear; here, now, this day, most people looked like mental cases. Even more desperate was the situation of women, who must go to extremes to elicit even the most transitory of glances. Some, it is true, were dressed demurely, although the effect was overborne by a sort of post-modern hauteur in which they were wont to give expression to their independence of thought, their autonomy, their self-conscious strength, their independence, their good ward-robe, etc., etc. Five minutes, that was all I asked, just five minutes to reason with them. One by one. In a narrow room. I recalled then a saying of Nietzsche's concerning women and the need for bull hide whips.

I could see youths, most of them wearing sneers and communication equipment strapped to their insolent heads. Suddenly I made an abrupt move, stopping myself just in time before kicking one of them, and not even the worst, kicking him I started to say, in his twenty-first century ass. Came then a negro with his shirt down to his groin, his pantaloons down to his knees, and his face tat-tooed in imitation of the statuary on Easter Island. But no, it wasn't tattooed after all! I wrote it down.

Given nerve enough and time, I could have emulsified the whole mass of them with one little spurt from Casper's magic device. And yet, when I considered the plight of earthlings and what they were made of (pus and lymph, intestines and shit entrapped in skin), and how that each of them was scheduled for death and disease and must toil away the best hours of each and every day, serfs dying by inches in office buildings, and considering one thing and another, the scarcity of love for example (we are speaking here of the real thing, and not just coital arrangements), bad weather and the cruel necessity of food and social co-operation, the horrors brought forth by change, and so forth and so on . . . Well! that was when my underlying weakness came to the surface, and I was near to feeling sorry for these people.

It was a temptation certainly, and yet I was able to fend it off. People must always be striving for transcendence, or else get out of the way of my colleagues and me. And be-sides, this evil place must go back to grass someday, supplying forage but for insects. I wept for the economists, the sociologists, the prime time talk show hosts who must then find other employment. And anyway, there was not a single individual in this or any other crowd who lacked the capacity to do away with him/herself.

Eight

All my life I have wanted to murder a beloved individual, and then to be seen grinning victoriously on television; instead I gathered my umbrella and some other things and stepped out into the rain. It was an appreciable distance to our preferred saloon, and I had thousands of yards to go before arriving at the door.

It was owing I suppose to my fastidious nature that we almost never congregated at my own apartment. I disliked cigars, or to find condensation rings left on my furniture through the agency of ice-cold drinks. Disliked people taking my books out of position and then prying them open where they night happen upon old letters or bills of currency deposited there by me. It was for that reason that we met these days in the above-cited restaurant called *Good Eats* where the customers were few and far between and the management entertained no evident hostility to intellectuals of our kind. On the contrary, given more maturity, a more interesting personality, and a few cultural acquirements, he might almost have been an associate of our little group.

"To put it plainly," said K, once we had settled and had organized our arthritic limbs and had passed around a laminated menu of about the size of a tabloid newspaper, "to put it plainly, we must all of us regret that we weren't allowed to live out our lives in a better civilization than the one we see around us here today." (He motioned to the pianist, the cat, and finally the outside world in its current state. He had chosen, K, a mint liqueur served in a thimble-size cup with a precipitate in it. This man ate sparingly at all times, and his plate held nothing but an assortment of mostly denuded bones that might almost have belonged to a hummingbird.) "Isn't that what we want? A superior world? People dedicated to supernal concerns?"

He had expressed it about as succinctly as anyone could. No one demurred. The speaker now handed the floor to Casper, who pursued the conversation in a marginally less belligerent mode.

"Well hell yeah we want a better America! It's our duty! But it's absurd to imagine that *everyone* wants to be better. Or could."

I agreed, and the motion passed.

"Lucky if we could cause just ten percent to be better. And anyway, we're too old ever to know whether we succeeded or not."

"He's right."

"But it's our responsibility all the same."

"Five percent. Persuade just *five percent* and we could renew the world!"

"Possibly, possibly. An aristocracy of five percent shouldn't have much trouble agreeing on how others must behave."

"But that's what we got now!"

"Oh? You believe our present-day five percent are the best the country has? Basketball players and stock manipulators?"

Well, we had to laugh at that. The America five percent? And had ever a more degraded and self-serving coalition ever before existed? This was our collective view of those people.

"Gentlemen, I think we must substitute *our* five for *their* five, yes? To bring about the rule of wisdom and integrity?"

"Wait a minute. You think good people would be willing to throw away their lives on something as boring as that?"

"They *are* boring. And that's a fact."

"Actually, one person would be enough. If he be great enough."

"Exactly. And no need to be so goddamn tenderhearted with the others. That was Critias' mistake."

"OK, let's write it down: 'Latin to begin at age five. Greek at seven.' How about Chinese? They're getting awfully uppity these days."

"Chinese my ass! This is to be a *Western* society my friends. I'm talking Greek and German, for Christ's sakes. Plato. Botany. Engineering. The rest can very happily rot their brains out on pornography and beer. Sooner the better!"

(At those words I experienced an unaccustomed surge of spiritual excitement that started at the loins and worked its way outward to a person's very fingertips.)

"Just so long as I don't have to live next door to one."

We laughed. Said I: "And let them have large fancy houses. Thousand horsepower cars."

"New kinds of drugs."

"Women with multiple orifices."

"Football twenty hours a day."

K clapped hands and spun about. "How happy they shall be! But as for the *power*, we'll want to hold that real close to our chests."

Said then Casper in a dreamy, far-away voice that exposed how much he had been drinking: "These best people, they must be identified when they're young, and trained to their destination. Few will make it. A thousand, shall we say, out of four hundred million?"

"Thousand." (This man also had been drinking. Looking at him closely, I wasn't by any means so sure that *he'd* be among those selected. Truly, it might ultimately come down to just one of us in fact.)

"No, Greek at five. It's harder. Latin later."

"And we shall give great honor to our military, don't you agree? A separate caste. Remember how Alexander's veterans were the best troops in all the world even after they'd passed the age of seventy?"

"I'll be seventy in November," the bartender called over to us.

"Yes, we must muster our old men. What would they have to lose after all? Old men without wives?"

"Now this military y'all keep talking about," said the bartender, "how does that fit in with all this other stuff?"

We looked at him severely, till finally he took up his rag and commenced to hum while swiping the bar with expert strokes. He'd never be one of us.

We needed lots of argumentation before settling on our priorities, and by that time two of us were drunk. K and I agreed to usher the others back to their apartments. It was exactly 1:27 on that Thursday morning, a moment that some three-quarters of a century later was destined to be memorialized nation-wide with cannon fire and song.

Nine

With spring coming in, three of us fell sick, a consequence of the sight of pretty girls in April wearing scarves and lipstick. There was no longer any question in my mind but that these people were *deliberately* and *consciously* beautifying themselves in all sorts of ways. One could start at the toes, or the other way around, and never discover any human part that hadn't either been emphasized or minimized, covered with shellac, dusted with powders, and deodorized. But what did they actually look like underneath all that? Yes?

I tried not to look at them. Instead, running quickly through the list of English Kings, I kept my attention on the pavement. Never mind women, what was it that lay beneath the surface of the world and supported the city? A half-dozen corroded iron rods as thin as toothpicks, a few captured prisoners, and not much else.

The climate notwithstanding, my friends and I had no intention of wasting our time on women. As if it weren't foolish enough when time is running out to squander one's attention on brushing one's teeth, polishing one's shoes, or sitting in vain for long period on one's toilet. Accordingly, we gathered two nights later at that same bar and grill that depended upon us for that part of its revenue that the authorities had determined to be legal. The lights were out of order, the flypaper was bejeweled with corpses, and the jukebox loaded with the tunes of 1953. But even then we had to wait a while before Casper arrived and after getting into his glasses (one lens good and the other glass), began to examine the room with his unreliable eye.

"Over here Casper," we said. "About 20 degrees to the left."

He was a sorry-looking person in his spotted trousers and crumpled hat. His bitterness however, that was intact.

"Drink up!" we insisted.

"What *is* this? Jesus!"

"Just drink it, OK?"

"Blimey, but I had a bad dream last night. Dreadful. I'm just afraid I might forget it."

"And so you need to tell us about it, right? Before you forget. Alright, go ahead, we're listening, Howard and I."

"How about Earl?"

Earl, as he very well knew, had been called to the Research Triangle in North Carolina where a project was under way. They imagined, those people, that humans could be "scanned," producing a "blueprint" of a person's atomic structure which then could be forwarded on waves of light to parts of our domestic galaxy. Having found the right sort of moon or planet, a clone could then be put together out of the elements at hand. Incredibly, Earl thought so, too.

"Returning, if I may, to my dream, I thought I was back in college once again and had to take an important test."

"And?"

"But I couldn't find the building!"

"Oh, boy. OK, is there anyone out there who *hasn't* had that dream? Hm? Anyone?"

"And I couldn't find my pen neither!"

"Those dreams are just standard issue Casp. Anything else?"

"Why yes, I dreamt I was being chased by a bear, and my feet wouldn't move!"

"Feet? You only got one!"

"He just kept getting closer and closer, and it was like my feet, foot, was glued to the ground!"

Impossible not to laugh. He was by far the most adorable man in the crowd.

"And then I felt like I was falling from the top of one of those buildings. Now that is one sick feeling! You begin to realize that you're just going to keep on falling, maybe forever, and you don't know what's down there!"

"Drink up."

He lifted the beaker and drank. There were ashes in the fluid as also what appeared to be a monstrous amoeba climbing ever so slowly to the rim.

"Well I guess that's all I have to say. Tell about *your* dreams Howard. You won't, will you?"

"Me? My dreams are a bit more . . . rarified than yours."

"We knew they would be."

I ignored him. "Since you ask, I dreamt I was in a strange place and . . ."

"That's not a dream."

". . . dreamt that all things yet to come had taken place already. And history, you see, is but the modality by means of which the human mind brings order to what happened long ago in one fell moment outside of time."

"Good, good. How about you K, you had any brief dreams lately?"

"Me? Just that same old face glaring down at me from about two inches away."

"More beer!" Casper bawled out suddenly, awakening the barman. "We're done with dreams, so let's hear about your famous illnesses Howard. I bet I got more than you."

"You do *not* have more than me and never will. No one has or ever did."

"He doesn't want to talk about it."

"Since you ask once again, I'll say that my intestines were always a problem, and now I've lost another five inches to my proctologist. Shall I go on?"

"Not necessarily."

"I have six prescriptions, each for a different organ."

"Child's play. I have nine. OK, three of them are for the same problem."

"Which problem is that K?"

"And when I decide to die, all I have to do is just stop taking one of those pills. The pink one."

"Headaches, I have the most appalling headaches."

"Actually I used to play pretty good tennis. I know you don't believe that."

"Jesus. You people don't know the first thing about agony and pain! Try lying out in the middle of a rice paddy with a shattered thigh."

"I've never heard of a paddy like that."

"I once had six consecutive kidney stones in a row, all within a month."

"Oh, I'm impressed! Kidney stones. I've gotten so used to those that I've begun to miss them. Try lying out in a paddy with a bunch of gooks milling about."

"I recollect as when my wife had her baby. Something *you'll* never have to witness."

"You have no wife. And even fewer babies."

"I sit here with one eye and one leg, and have to listen to this?"

Etc.

We quibbled till half past two and then, taking the key (and concomitant responsibilities), we allowed the barman to decamp for his own two-room flat on the other side of Brooklyn. The time had come to be serious and to regulate our plans for the future. Itself, the tap was flowing freely, and the beer was black.

"You can talk all you want," one of us said, "but we still haven't settled upon our primary purpose. Why for example do we have to kill so many people?"

"Revenge, that's a great part of it. Surely you remember all those people studying business administration while we were doing Greek? I've always been proud of that."

"You were proud ere you were born."

We drank. Characteristic of people of our maturity, time was passing at an unconscionable rate. For all that I could say, the twenty-second century might already be in progress even as we sat talking. I rose to fetch another beer, and by the time I returned the amoeba had escaped.

"No, I move that we take on elected officials first of all."

"He's right. Anyone who can win a popular election in this country doesn't deserve to go on living."

"A caste system, we agree on that. Good people in control." (Sudden he jumped up and ran off to urinate, the third time within as many minutes.)

"Not so sure I want to be in control of anybody."

"Oh? And we're not so sure that you're one of the good persons."

"Naw, he's alright. Good enough anyway."

"May I speak?'

"Not necessarily."

"We must define just what sort of society is most propitious . . ."

"Did we say you could speak?"

". . . most propitious for the emergence of spiritual qualities. We think of Medieval times, and people's assurance in the availability of supernal values. No, no, I'm not promoting any particular religion. I *am* promoting a world in which people understand that they themselves are not terribly important." (This from a man with such great big pores in his nose that the thing appeared to harbor worms.)

"Wisdom. Wisdom and knowledge. Wisdom, knowledge, beauty, and the place we go to when we have died."

"He really believes that. Don't you Howard?"

"I believe in the place whence came Mahler's Eighth."

"It came from his brain, I've always thought."

"Not a whit. How could beauty set up housekeeping in that tiny space? Sorry boys, it's a real thing, beauty, and not just an opinion. It originates in a real place, and will subsist forever, long after the youngest of us has leapt off the world into some other passing universe."

"You're an abstract man Howard. Just think of the metaphysician you might have made!"

"Remember this, that it's not Mahler, but Mahler's Eighth that matters. He was simply the conduit chosen by the Graces. He who puts his faith in mere human beings sups on rubbish. Somebody said that."

"I'd like to put an end to some of your rubbish. That would be my preference."

"People like us, artists and so forth, we alone have been authorized to stroll the ocean floor in search of ancient coins."

"Oh, Jesus. More of that?"

"Rubies and coins. The sun is made of ambrosia, but only we have tongues long enough."

"OK, that'll do it for me. I'm out of here."

Ten

On a Friday about two months later, I was given a message from Earl in which that most assiduous of men had listed the two-hundred-twelve individuals most responsible for the influx of non-Caucasians into our country. The names were immediately recognizable, most of them, though I was surprised by an addendum of another two dozen more who had been operating under anglicized names. Some were dwelling "under our noses," so to speak, in law-abiding neighborhoods with gated fences and twenty-four-hour police protection. But to gather all 212 + 24 together in one narrow spot and liquidate the entire crowd at once . . . No, by God, we'd have to chase them down one by one.

"And we don't even know if that gadget will work!" said one of my friends, can't remember which.

"'Gizmo,' not 'gadget.' Don't know if the *gizmo* actually works."

"OK, gizmo. But will it work?"

We had come together in Earl's apartment where to my surprise Casper had lately taken up quarters. She had a special sympathy, had Earl's wife, for Casper's disabilities, and I fully expected that he would shortly be adopted into the family. Myself, I owned far too many books to be sharing my limited space, and then, too, I adored my privacy perhaps more than I should. My address was hard to find, and the walls too thick for the passage either of conversation or gunfire. But enough about these matters, walls and so forth. I've digressed.

As mentioned, we had come together in Earl's apartment, and after a serving of tea and cinnamon toast from the hand of Earl's excellent woman, we began at last to debate how best and how soon to employ the gadget.

"Maybe we should postpone it," Earl suggested. "Till June or July."

"Interesting. You think it might not work, don't you?"

"Not work? Of course it works!"

"You're afraid it won't work, and that will be why you keep moving the date."

"The date, as you call it, is perfectly well capable of moving itself."

"Afraid it won't work, and so he retreats into his dark library and just sits there."

"My library, as you call it, *has all the illumination* it needs."

"Sits there ruminating about nothing."

"Alright, sometimes it's about nothing. But sometimes it's about the most pressing issues of the day!"

"He's getting upset. Look at him."

"It's true, Earl, that you've been looking a little bit . . . how shall I say? Is atrabilious the word? What, losing your desire to kill people?"

"Not me."

Earl's wife broke in. "He doesn't have to kill people if he doesn't want to! And once he's recovered, he'll probably be killing more than all of you put together!"

Despite my hesitation, we set a time, May 22nd to be precise, the anniversary of the disappearance of Casper's wife. It was I who I mooted the possibility of rural Vermont for our initial trial. A tiny state, narrower than most, the area was known for its painterly qualities, its hills and maples, its famous poet, and the world's worst weather.

Eleven

By the end of May I had received my first driving lesson from Casper along with the use of his car. Appropriately, the vehicle was an old one, providing neither a CD player, nor geodetic positioning device, nor air conditioner, nor a good many other needless things. Wait, did I just now undervalue CD players? For me, that was essential equipment, unless I wanted to endure ten or fifteen hours without music. Accordingly, I borrowed Earl's battery-driven player and loaded the car with Wagner and Ravel, a bit of early Shostakovich, the *Psalmus Hungaricus* of Kodály, additional Wagner, and more than just a tiny sample of several other people as well. I considered these to be the best parts of a piece, where "pieces" are defined as parts of a whole.

The day was adequate, which is to say neither very cloudy nor the other way around. My driving skills were poor—I admit that—and in the beginning I had some dangerous tendencies having to do with steering and some of the "fine print," so to speak, that would probably have been found in driving manuals. For fuel, I chose a new experimental stuff derived from animal wastes and roses, an expensive hydrocarbon that gave off an uncanny odor.

I was alone, but the car was loaded with music, a telephone, a suitcase with two of my better outfits in it, silk ties from ------------ of London, fresh underwear, shaving equipment, a loaded .32 caliber Beretta affixed to my ankle with electric tape, and a paper bag holding two "Reuben" sandwiches made of cheese, ham, bacon, sauerkraut, and other ingredients that can't be described without exciting a person's appetite, all of it named after a certain former dictator of controversial memory.

I carried maps of course, walking boots, a copy of one of Perdue's better novels, a jug of wine, and in the glove compartment a blond wig and half a dozen vials of the sort of cosmetics used in disguises. I had an umbrella, a Frasier repair manual (acquired after much effort), and some $3,200 in unmarked bills. But all of this fades away into entire inconsequentiality when compared and contrasted with what by all measures was to prove the most sought-after invention since the development of DIY retrogendering kits.

This last-mentioned article fit easily on that rather narrow shelf that lies between the rear window and the back
seat, a wasted area usually, save when young children use
it for sleeping. Viewed from behind, the gizmo must have
looked like a shoebox with four choice lines of Baccylides
on it. But even with all this, it still required me better than
a full hour to drive through a Honduran enclave that had
been sectioned off by the police some two years previously. I moved slowly past a landmark structure where once I
had enrolled in a scholarly enclave convoked to debate the
syntactical vagaries of third tranche Oxyrhynchian papyri.
Recently the city had begun to import quantities of basalt,
mica, soybeans, petroleum, and especially water; once
past the storage bins, I needed less than another hour to
move through the outlying slops of The World City.

I was responsible for a small mishap in ------------, but
the other car was too awkwardly positioned to give chase.
Casper's vehicle had been organized to accommodate a
one-legged person, making it difficult for a full human
being to captain the thing. And anyway the Frasier already
bore a great many dents and chaffed places. Three hours
out of Queens, I pulled over, enjoyed a sandwich, and
smoked two cigarettes. The weather was improving, which
is to say it had finally decided whether to be cloudy or
clear. As always in such matters, I wanted things to be
more *decisive*, whether for ill or the other way around.

You will have noticed how the same piece of music im-
pacts a person differently according to listener's mood? I
was enjoying an early recording of Chausson when a pa-
trolman pulled up and for a long time drove abreast of me.
Did he object to the Confederate Flag furling from the
passenger side window? I smiled, a tactic that delayed the
crucial moment until I had crossed the county line and
was able to turn loose of the Beretta in my right hand.

Lake Champlain proved larger than I had expected. I
applied to the ferryman who however refused responsibil-

ity for an antique car more valuable than his insurance coverage. For one brief moment I was tempted to use the gizmo on him; instead, I had to turn about and travel a good forty miles out of my path. I had determined from the start to reach the area about Mt. Mansfield where a certain famous love affair had worked itself out in old times.

But first a bookstore, a compulsive temptation for persons of my sort. A couple of strange old books and a tin of maple syrup with a colorful and historically important label on it, these alone would have compensated me for stopping.

I parked, a more difficult operation than usually understood. At first there had been an old man sitting on the porch who however rose and went quickly inside as I struggled with the controls of this all-too-stubborn car. Such was the landscape of Vermont that I had ended up about two inches from a precipice that fell into a very pretty lake. Here I opened my medicine bag and after taking two valiums and a green raniform pill for unremembered needs, I strode with some arrogance into the wayside "bookstore," or tourist attraction really, simulating a log cabin. In fact the "cabin" had two antennae on the roof, a swimming pool out back and once inside, had all manner of electronic devices, a pool table, and a television set as large almost as my bedstead back in New York.

"Tourist trade must be wonderful these days!" I said, smiling. "Where're the books actually?"

The hostess was a bitter-looking quantity devoid of make-up and dressed in cast-off clothes. And yet she was young enough still to be ovulating, the stage where clothes and make-up were normally expected. A long time had gone by since she had offered her love to anyone, causing the stuff to cumulate and turn her into a humpback person. Slowly, very slowly—(I divined that her marriage, had ever she had one, hadn't been happy)—very slowly, as I was saying, she lifted from her stool and guided me to a vestibule where some few score of rubbishy books lay, not on shelves, but in one unsteady pile about ten feet tall in vertical height.

"I want that one," said I humorously, indicating the bottommost volume.

She never responded. She should have been using a brassiere, and her clothen shoes did not appear to be a pair. Leaving her, I pulled forward an ancient chair and by mounting it was able to read the spines of some of the dog books, books about flowers, recipe collections, Sears catalogs, women's novels, and other related material that exposed the intellectual level of the place.

"I would have thought," said I, "that you'd at least have a copy or two of the poetry of ------------." (I mentioned his famous name.)

"Who?"

Useless. In fact I was about ready to give up my inspection when I perceived a waterlogged tome in cracked binding. The thing was in such neglected condition, it might be good.

"May I remove just this one volume?" I respectfully inquired. "And have a look at it?"

"Might as well look at it," she said, "since you already got it in your hand." (I had left the gizmo in the car.)

In the event, the book turned out to be a certain seventeenth-century grimoire that I had been pursuing more or less fanatically for twenty years.

"Jesus!" I submitted. "Look at this!"

She never responded. The thing had woodcuts in it, also a private letter (written in German) left there all those years ago. Between the pages I discovered a dried flower of some description together with a smattering of perhaps twenty very tiny little seeds. Earl, the best biologist in New York, would know how to cultivate these miniscule things and bring them back to life again. What else did the book contain? Unrevealed information on the assassination of Henri IV? Bills of ancient currency?

"I think I'd like to purchase this," I admitted.

"Would? About ready to fall apart, looks to me."

"Oh? Well you know, people like me. We have a weakness for this sort of thing."

"It figures. Soon as you walked in. I'm asking four hundred for it."

"Jove! That's high, don't you think?"

"You'll pay it. And I'll throw in a quart of that there maple syrup, if that's what it is."

I did pay, and in return the woman helped to turn the car around and aim it in the right direction. This Vermont countryside was a very superior sort of thing and much enhanced by little red barns, split rail fencing, cattle, and other touristic inducements. I passed a small goat operation, orchards, and an austere-looking man in a straw hat leading a shoat by a string. So gorgeous a locale sitting just outside the emanations of The World City. Life is full of such comparisons and contrasts.

I drove forward slowly through that excelsior landscape that seemed to conform note for note with the second suite of Ravel's *Daphnis*. The music also had "pastures" in it (speaking figuratively of two very different media), whilst meanwhile a veil of smoke and fog had descended from the mountaintops. Assailed from both directions, I began to have that feeling that stands in lieu of religion for me, when beauty is in surfeit. It was too much, a good experience driven to extremes, I just might have to faint. And that was the moment I caught Beauty herself, a thoroughgoing monster, larger than the moon, grinning down upon me from just behind the ridge.

I was lucky. How many other geniuses have been given even just one such glimpse? I could name three, four at best. I will say this, too, that not even the boldest among us would dare drive those same miles when *au-*

tumn be in flower.

But I had been wrong about the fog; actually that was *night* itself coming on. I bethought me then of your so-called *chemical titrations*, when one substance has met and at last overwhelmed another, an obvious reference here to the diurnal tournament 'tween night and day. I reached for my revolver. Up ahead a raccoon or some like beast had stepped out into the highway and was targeting me with radioactive eyes. And then, as if that weren't enough, I had come into view of a roadside advertisement that sparkled blindingly in the headlights

Soon I would need a meal, a drink, a pillow for my poor head. At least my fuel was still in good supply, relatively speaking, and like me, the car still refused to capitulate to the ordeals and disappointments of old age. I could have taken this antique to a dealer and come away with lots of money, so much was it in demand by rich collectors. I passed a field of sorghum, and then a tall narrow home teetering under gales of anti-matter. Pushing my mind forward a few thousand years, I could pretty well foresee the doom awaiting this and all other Vermonts the world over. Life is woeful. I let loose of my revolver. A motel came flying up at me at thirty-five miles an hour.

I never stopped, not till I descried a really desperate-looking restaurant—my kind of place!—with just two people in it. I parked skillfully, fairly skillfully, and switched the motor off. Always in love with neon, it did me good to go to the window and see three examples of that sort of illumination, a granular stuff delivered in slow-moving quanta that could almost be counted. The waitress, if she wanted to satisfy my stereotype, should be about forty-two years old, divorced, overweight, with at least two unregistered children waiting patiently for her back at the house. She would be wearing a little white cap bearing the name of the establishment. She would of course have missed out on those epiphanies and aesthetic realizations that make life acceptable, even exciting at times. There is much to be said for Japanese movies, for organic chemistry, and Grecian literature, but no chance soever that this woman ever would know aught about any of it. I admit it, I felt a sort of sorrow for her and all her analogs everywhere.

In the event, she was not much more than thirty-five, and her cap was blue not white. There were two other customers in the place, both of them intimidated to silence by my entrance, my presentation, my suit and shoes, my arrogance and combed silver hair that still showed the plow marks of the comb. That hair of mine, not only was it more abundant than any of theirs, it was as glossy as a silver trout, or sun glyphs on running water, or an arctic mink who had turned out glossier than normal. The cashier smiled, causing me to bow (slightly) and reciprocate with a six (on a ten scale) smile of my own.

Once everyone had settled down, I saw the place was not quite as dispiriting as I had wanted. To reach the darkest part I had to march past five empty and two occupied booths before finding the place reserved by providence for me. Seen from across the room, I have no doubt but that I was a striking, even a worrying sight. And then, too, my habit when among inferior people was to make no slightest movement of any kind, as if I had been sculpted out of onyx. The waitresses were disputing among themselves as to which of them would have to come and see me. It ended with the girl with the flaxen hair.

"A Tom Collins please. But with vodka instead of rum."

"Yes, sir. We have beer."

I looked at her severely. Her mind was weak.

"As you wish," I said. "Very well, let me have two lamb chops garnished with butter and water cress. And the apposite vegetables, too, if you please."

"We have pork crops."

"As you wish."

She ran to fetch them. If only the whole world were as obedient, we wouldn't be talking about gizmos and the like. I had positioned myself just next to a narrow window that looked out by starlight upon another of those landscapes that bring tears to people like me—a sixteenth-century scene with hand-built homes and well-mown fields, a collapsed barn here and a new one there, fine libraries in every parlor, a cheerful wife with merry bosoms, herds of kine and/or cattle defended by unsleeping dogs with eyes stretched wide. And this: How could the vision be as wonderful as it was while the people who infested it be what they inevitably were?

The chops proved tasty, especially when enriched with some 200 grains of freshly-milled pepper. Itself, the butter had melted down into a fund of juice into which I was wont to dip the remains of my light-crust biscuit. The milk, too (chosen in lieu of beer), was rich and cool and sometimes—I admit it—I might also dip the crust (but only an inch or two), into that as well! Finally came desert, a cherry compote with sweet cream on top, followed by an invoice for fifty-seven dollars.

"Yikes!" I said.

"We take cards," she said, her face hardening.

With human material such as this, I might as well have been back in New York City. And that of course was when I caught sight of myself in the window. I looked, and probably I still do, like a Manhattan doorman whose nephew had run off to Bulgaria to avoid Federal taxes on a failed laundromat.

Twelve

I couldn't sleep, nor could have anyone attempting to do so in a room full of mosquitoes. The pillow was misshapen, had an acorn in it, and I missed the indentions in my quondam bed. Finally, at just past 1:00 a.m. in the morning (speaking pleonastically), I urinated, arose, and shaved (though not necessarily in that order), and brought together my guns and clothes. I had no choice but to void my bowels as well, admittedly a strange way to use the little bit of time left to me on earth. Completing that project, I chose to quit the motel without confronting the proprietor, a bald man, quite unbalanced, who had excited my sympathy by virtue of his great age. Moving with stealth, I actually did achieve all those aims save one.

By night, the road appeared both longer and narrower than it should. After proceeding without mishap for some minutes, I suddenly pulled off and sheltered beneath a largish tree of some kind, hoping to avoid detection by an aircraft, or "drone," so-called, moving slowly overhead. The state of Vermont, normally so respectful of authority, had been cited in recent reports for a disproportionate number of same race matrimonies. Off in the distance in the far southeast I caught sight of what either was a building or a haystack going up in flame.

I had been cautioned about sleeping while driving, wherefore I slowed at the next tavern and contrived to park between two other vehicles much more modernistic than mine. The place was still open even at this hour, but when I went to the window and saw the character of the people . . . I paced back hurriedly to the Kaiser and after forcing it into gear, continued deeper into the mystic black night.

The sun, when it came, came exactly in the predicted location. Larger than Europe, the object appeared "out of round," owing I suppose to the pull of the horizon. I couldn't risk looking at it for long, lest I wanted to lose my sight. Instead I took two brief glances at the "worms" (as laymen call them), huge white worms writhing in agony on the surface.

Again I pulled off, this time to allow my eyes to adjust.

A car was coming, a dark blue manufacture interrupting the privacy of what I now considered my own personal highway. Seeing me stranded there, would the driver stop and offer help? Help? I had rather be dead. In fact the villain rushed on past without a pause. Finally, suffering from lack of sleep, I put on the piano concerto of Fröderline and stretched out on the front seat. There followed then about thirty uncomfortable minutes of which not more than five constituted actual sleep.

I was old, and life was running through my fingers. Gathering my nerve, I looked at myself in the rearview mirror. I had passed almost the whole of my life thinking of myself as either a young or a middle age man, and now this. Perhaps I should arm the gizmo at this point and eliminate myself. Or, perhaps I should get back on the road again.

I arrived at Brent Forest at just after ten and after putting on a cordial smile and showing my papers, drove unhurriedly past the tobacco detector. I spotted one of the new pleasure stalls, an upholstered cell with a hole in the wall. I avoided a squirrel loitering in the road, a bicyclist, and then a spate of tourist shops painted all colors. I should have ignored these places, and would surely have done so but for a bookstore (!) with helium-filled balloons out front. I entered the place, having preliminarily brought the car to a stop and extracting the key. The custodian was a male in bib trousers, a mature sort of person pedaling on a sewing machine. All my life I have loved the sight of old-time professions still being practiced. Two years ago I spied a cobbler, a leathery man toiling away in that cluttered little room at the rear of his shop.

I was allowed to do my browsing without assistance. A well-organized business, the books had been set out in order of color and size. I hurried to the earliest of them, a nineteenth-century novel writ by a society woman dressed in a hat that resembled a birdcage. I replaced this book gingerly and then to my astonishment drew out another copy of that same volume on witchcraft and magic that I had so proudly and so recently come to possess. Only the price was different—two and a half dollars compared to four hundred. No doubt as I went on I could expect to find still other copies scattered along the roadbed.

Back on the road again! The sun was in a sorry state, its powers much curtailed by flights of crows passing across the face. It's true that I had been listening to some really fine music, and true, too, that the landscape in this region was infinitely superior to the people who hadn't hesitated to defile it with their industries, their billboards, and houses. They deserved every good thing that came their way—they believed this. In fact the whole state would have to be evacuated once I came to power. Smiling at the thought, I nearly crashed into a post-modern automobile monopolizing the on-coming lane.

In obedience to my arthritis I stopped again, exited the automobile, and walked back and forth for a minute. The escrubilator was where I had left it, but the car itself continued to sneak forward even after I had taken out the keys. Lest someone come and offer to help, I left the road, ignited a cigarette, and moved toward the roadside forest where the trees stood so close, one to another, that a person of my size and type would have to take detours and even at times to reverse himself if he wished to make progress.

The woods were bright and green, and I had yards to go before I peed. Or if not yards, a couple of feet anyway, where a narrow earthen road strayed away into the unknown. I took that road. My nerves were poor and not even *two* cigarettes (tell no one!) did ought to assuage them. I also washed down a half-inch of my raspberry wine before I noticed that the berries had settled to the bottom and begun to putrefy. The path, too, was disappointing, and ere long began to taper in upon itself until the weeds and branches were pressing at both sides. Here I stopped and after squandering a minute or two in deep thought, began to force my way deeper into the forest.

I traveled far. Far when measured against the difficulty of the route, I should have said. In fact I was passing over ground that had perhaps never experienced the footfall of any white American. My mind jumped back to around 1500 or 1600, when red Indians had likely passed this way. I had never forgot something told by Parkman, that these foolish tribes, not understanding that winter was bound to come again, had neglected to stow away their nuts and corn against that contingency. Of course I was just mentally drifting at that moment, postponing the deed that was to inscribe my name in history.

By 2:09 I had come to the edge of an extensive dairy farm, a utopian establishment with white fencing, sweet grass, and scores of smiling cattle all facing in the same direction. The family house, situated far away, was built of brick and had a balcony on it. I looked for but could not immediately discover any fanciful little gazebo with a pretty girl in crinoline reading poetry. And instead of horses and carriages, the place had two shiny cars out front, both of them undoubtedly costly but neither with a value like mine.

I did *not* intend to disintegrate the cows, or building, nor barn neither, nor even the tin rooster posturing atop the weather vane. With the clock now approaching 2:45, my suit had endured a lot of thorns, one of them actually yanking out my tie and leaving it to dangle. Suddenly I froze, remembering that I had left the gizmo behind where any passing clown could lift it from the car and run away with it.

You will have guessed that I did in fact recover the thing, reaching the car at 2:58 and then returning to my

location just minutes later. I was old, getting older, and
my mental procedures had slowed to the speed characteristic of ordinary geniuses of the usual kind. Might not this
be a good place for dying? And to be found centuries
hence, a skeleton holding on for dear life, irony not intended, to an unexplained instrument full of wires and the
refried brain of a rhesus monkey? This put me in mind of
a recent excavation in which the bones of a Bronze Age
couple had been found entwined in an eternal embrace. I
was drifting.

To abbreviate, I soon happened upon a cowshed, or
corncrib, or some like structure that had been let to fall
apart. About fifteen feet high at its tallest part, the building offered a pretty good target for a person carrying a
weapon of uncertain power. The place had spiders, a discarded automobile battery, a decayed leather harness, and
a trove of letters put away in a cardboard box. Should I
have read those letters? In any case the stamps were gone,
which might have been worth a lot at today's auction prices.

Day was drawing on, and soon it would be three
o'clock. The woods were dank and deep, and owing to all
the fallen walnuts and sweet gum balls, I was in constant
danger of falling to the ground. And yet I was at this moment the most important person in the world. Accordingly I drew off about forty paces, withdrew the gizmo from
its polished container, and pressed it tightly to my ear. If I
had expected to pick up sounds like those emanating from
a vacant sea shell, or like the stridulations of a cricket, or
the ululations of Arab women at a funeral . . . No, it
sounded like a far-away voice recycling a radio show of
seventy years ago. The electronics were complicated, and
it would need the combined talents of at least two of us to
explain them.

Absent the sun, the device would have had no more
utility than a tangle of wires and software and a few other

science things. But *with* the help of the sun, this ingenious device immediately reported back the precise coordinates of the target in all the dimensions needed to define its cosmic location with perfect precision and then stash that information away eternally in the left lobe of its rhesus brain.

My time was drawing nigh. Above, two ravens had been joined by a third, and the whole trifecta seemed to triangulating me with evil intent. I smoked a cigarette. Tried to urinate but couldn't, or anyway not without a lot of patience. It was now just 3:27 in the afternoon, the same fateful sort of moment as when Wagner, Berlioz, and Gounod found themselves sitting next to each other at the premiere of *Faust*, a matinee performance apparently. Or as when Adam took the apple, or Abelard elected to leave Héloise behind. That was when I pushed the button.

Thirteen

I never really cared very much for those authors who will break away from a story at the most crucial place. But to revert back to the story in progress, nothing happened. All of us were failures, especially Casper who had accepted overall responsibility for the expected performance of our little mechanism. *Nothing happened.* The ravens continued their obnoxious noises while the great white puffy clouds went about their time-hallowed permutations. One cloud indeed looked like a famous paleontologist pictured in a certain old book of mine, a standard text riddled with comical but at the same time very interesting misconceptions. Ought l pack my equipment, load the car, and point said vehicle in the right direction?

No such thing, not with the building beginning to groan and make anguished noises as the ionization gathered force. It trembled, it groaned, and ten seconds later was transformed into a structure made of *water*, as that layman might have supposed. It was like a murdered person who had continued to stand upright for a short period. I could see old bottles and letters and dried-up paint brushes turning into a pool of molecules that had lost their integrity. It couldn't and didn't endure for long, and by 3:42 the whole mess had been reduced to a shallow puddle covered over, it appeared, with the blue-green algae familiar to us from biology class. And so this is how the world ends, not with a whimper but the breaking of valance bonds.

No need to explain my return voyage to New York City. Except to mention that by 4:17 I had managed to turn the car about and was riding at high speed direct into the decaying sun. I had put on two discs of chamber music, good stuff that sorted perfectly with my tobacco habit and the remains of my pocket flask. It would be dark by the time the liquor was exhausted, and I had reason to fear I might all-too-easily capitulate to my wish for sleep and oblivion and interesting dreams. In fact I was driving well, sometimes even intimidating people much younger than me. I was too shrewd actually to stop for hitchhikers, based upon what I had heard about these people, and at my wonted speed, none had the least possibility of chasing me down. Having then come into a quaint little village just as the sun was going down, I moved slowly through a crowd of generic youths who had been waiting there since the beginning in order to insult my car. Not wanting to use the gizmo over so trivial a matter, I turned at the following intersection and continued west.

It was full dark by 7:16, and the sky was full of foreign bodies. I detected one of the country's larger satellites passing overhead, the window full of faces. I would hate to give up these sights once death possessed me, and never mind all the bad stuff—should I provide a list?—all the bad stuff I yearned to escape. For instance to have fallen into a good civilization at the very moment putrefaction was setting in. Business and commerce, whole lives wasted in office buildings. Sophistication instead of the naiveté in which every day seems new and strange. And in short, I hated it.

The next village was smaller than its reputation, and within a minute or two I had reentered the black night with its stars and other appointments. The roadside litter was exiguous in a state where so few negroes dwelled. Even so I noted a couple of items that might excite the archeologists of the future. Just then a tavern came up on the left. Not a place for scholars, judging by the motorcycles, the bumper stickers, and the individual lying in the yard. Two fuzzy blood-red lights revealed the town's worst people hunched along the bar. Could I blame them? No doubt their occupations were boring beyond all description, and after certain years had come and gone, they had thrown up their hands and come to this.

I drove until 9:00 p.m. and continued on. Finally I had no alternative but to pull over, a maneuver that put me near to a gasoline filling station about twenty miles outside of Foulks where right away a phalanx of young people came forward to marvel at Casper's car. I had decided to disintegrate the first person who dared pronounce the word "cool," but in the event I had enough to do with filling the fuel, paying the man, and then getting down on the ground to retrieve the lid. Not that it was young people only; I was also approached by an older person who wanted to *buy* my ancient car. Waiting for things to settle, I entered the station, invested in a Moon Pie, a small Mountain Dew, and a tube of prescription toothpaste containing two percent of serotonin reuptake inhibitors. The men's room proved an unlikable place (urine on the floor) with an appalling epigraphy from floor to ceiling. Needless to say, the authors of those inscriptions had resolutely refused to use the blackboard provided for their convenience. To disremember the experience, I returned to the car where yet another Vermonter or New York man—how to distinguish?—had taken it upon himself—New Yorkers do dress somewhat better—had presumed to open the door so as better to read the dials and palpate the upholstery. He wanted to talk about it; instead I moved back out of conversational range and after orienting myself in the desired direction, succeeded in driving away without calling any further attention down upon myself.

I have always enjoyed crossing state and county boundaries, a time-honored method for escaping legal jurisdictions. I might be in Vermont, I might not. Or at my age, I might be in New Hampshire for all that I could confidently assert. In any case, I no longer put much credence in geography, or time, or any other category that imperiled my concentration on more noble matters, beauty for example, or hatred for imperfect things. Hatred? Already I could see the profile of New York City looming near.

Fourteen

It has been seen that I was approaching New York City. Those who have not had to earn a living in that place, they should know that New Yorkers are not normal people. They talk to feminists; they can't sleep. Many of them eat shit. Having forsaken the place just thirty-eight hours earlier, now I was home again. There were, of course, no cultural relics to improve the view, no monument to Edgar Poe for instance, far less to Oswald or James Earl Ray. Running through Queens, I stopped from time to time better to examine the people loitering on street corners, the architecture, music coming from the cars, and all the other realia that made the place what it was, a national set-aside boycotted alike by birds and animals of the more evolved type.

I should have driven straight to my apartment, and did. A small boy had been caught on my security camera, but other than for that, no one had actually entered the apartment during my absence. It is true that I had forgotten to fodder my chameleons, and the alpha male was snarling back at me from the northeastern corner of the enormous containment tank. However I soon put all that to rest with six frozen crickets and a few eyedroppers of thrice-distilled water. I might be an awful person in some respects, but I refused absolutely to supply my animals with New York "water," a stuff recycled so many times that it had been assigned its own position in the Periodic Table. Nor was that the only reason I considered this town the most fragile in all America.

Believe me when I say that I tried to sleep. My cozy apartment comprised 1,220 square feet of space, and yet a single active insect could obviate every inch. But even this was nothing compared to the metallic noise of the gizmo running through tables of hundred-digit cosign values about ten inches from my poor head.

I was nervous. I had seen what that thing (escrubilator) could do, and I was nervous. Rising and peeing, I took two Klonopin tablets of five mg each, a liver pill, a baby aspirin, and a Tom Collins made with cinnamon and rum. I changed sheets, and after opening the bedroom door and checking in both directions, I trod on down to my library and gathered up a book on particle physics, confident it would bring me sleep. My apartment had just one window, and the bars were too close together for any but a child. Therefore I needn't expect danger from that direction

All these considerations were quite unnecessary. Truth was, I was in possession of the most portentous invention since the development of language, or circular wheels, or fissile materials. But were I absolutely certain that the society I desired would be best for everyone and not just me? Or best anyway for the best? I thought about it, finally answering "yes" to the last question while retracting the first. It was now almost six o'clock, and soon the sun, a greenish remnant each day a little smaller, would lift the veil on New York City. (It is true that in places without high buildings, dawn comes earlier than this. Indeed I have seen locations in this conurbation where it never comes at all.) And anyway I was pretty sure by this time that I was just about ready to abandon the bed and get into my clothes.

To start, I drove the Frasier down to a certain famous delicatessen, entered in dignity, and then padded back to that dark cubicle in the rear where, here too, sunlight seldom entered. Still just half-awake, I enjoyed a cup of Third World coffee and a robust cream roll with six strawberries and two, or perhaps three, cherries on top, an unusual but appealing combination, as I am willing to concede. No one is more willing to give credit where it is deserved. I'm thinking particularly of darkened restaurants with candles and strawberries, and the sort. Indeed I might have stayed in that place the entire morning, except for a mixed party of prospering businesspussies with plasticized faces. They held degrees from northeastern colleges—one could be sure of that—and enjoyed bloated salaries. I had left the escrubilator in my apartment. Their legs, all eight of them, had however become disorganized in the process, and in one case a person had crossed her right limb with her neighbor's left. How lovely were they in their prissy little shoes and high-cost make-up! (I knew better. Ever seen a woman's abdomen opened up for surgery?) In fact they were but a few hundredweight of pus and excrement held together in colored dresses.

I returned to my apartment, released the trip wire, brushed my teeth, and urinated at greater length than normal. I was no bargain either, what with my "face," so-called, that more and more was coming to resemble my chameleons'. Amazing that I could still travel on legs worn down by now to the thinness of a hen's. Years had gone by since last I had dared look at my full self in the mirror.

 Having gathered up my bedside book, my cigarettes, my lucky coin, and the gizmo, I returned to the Kaiser and managed to exit the parking lot. The sun was what it was—it always was—and had found a point of entry between two or more adjacent buildings. On that showing, one might have thought it a painting by Munch exposed suddenly from behind a cloud. Or, he might think someone had tossed a gigantic egg against the sky, or that it were a hole in the firmament, or an exploded bomb. But far more likely than any of that, probably he would think it was the sun.

 I drove slowly down an avenue pullulating with men in suits who had rather be at home in bed. Really, wouldn't your average person prefer to be feeding cattle, or working at a forge, or rubricating medieval manuscripts? Truly we had come a long way from when most people were mostly unhappy most of the time, down to now, when it was *everybody*, and *all* the time.

 I had forgotten Earl's exact address, but found the place at last among a maze of little workshops—upholsterers, glove manufactures, hypnotists, rose merchants, college preparation tutors, and the like, a comfortable site for people like my friend and his pneumatic wife. To reach the man's entry I had to go up two unsound flights of stairs and then down again into a very brief halfway ending up as a place for mops and brooms and an obsolete fuse box used for pharmaceutical deliveries. Here I turned sharply to the left and, in obedience to our agreed code, knocked three times, vigorously.

 The man had been laboring at his desk, a pleasing sight, altogether meet for the type he was. Somehow the varlet had come into possession of a World War I water-cooled Vickers 303 capable of throwing 900 rounds per minute of uninterrupted employment. An intimidating instrument, this artifact from an earlier age stood in the corner pointing at the door. We shook briefly. His hand was perhaps a bit too *fatigué* for a revolutionary's, and he had an ingrown wedding ring strangling the life out of the traditional digit.

"Want a drink?" he asked.

"Of course."

"Good. Bring me one, too, will you?"

The kitchen was a mess, but his wife was not. To holster just one of her mammaries a man would need both hands. And then, too, her hips and other apparatus were nothing to sneeze at either.

"So rare," I said, "for a woman to be blessed in *both* regions."

"Well maybe I just try harder."

"Jesus. You know, I believe you could handle all four of us."

"At your age? I could handle a thousand."

I chose to say no more on that topic at this time. The liquor was stored in the bookcase where a person could get at it, and although the inventory had declined, a fundamental amount remained in easy reach. He had been working diligently, Earl had, and had finally uncovered perhaps ninety percent of the names of those who had authorized the replacement of the country's Caucasian peoples.

"I've brought the gizmo," I said. "Maybe you could be in charge of it for a while. Makes me nervous."

He stopped writing. The woman was standing in the doorway with a worried expression.

"What?"

"Nervous. And yet it works real well."

"You say that to me?"

"Of course you have to let it warm up at first."

"What, did you try it out on a child or something?"

"Child! Ha! No, I used a building."

"Oh shit."

"No, no, no. Nobody was in it."

"He says nobody was in it."

"Well, that's a relief. A small one, but still a relief. Christ, Howard, it might be months before we've even agreed on a target!"

"And no children, OK?" his wife added.

Impossible not to laugh. This was the reason, apart from the genius problem, why no woman had been invited to the team.

I needed an hour to tell what I had done, how I had brought back an interesting book while also reducing a hundred-year-old barn down to the sort of material more usually found clinging to the bottom of a person's shoes.

"It were in the deep woods," I said, "and it'll be years before anyone notices what was done."

"I see. Does K know about this? And that other fellow?"

"No, I came to you first, since you'll be taking charge of the gizmo."

"No!" the woman said. "We don't need no stinking grizbo!" (Impossible not to laugh. My own mother used to say things like that.)

He seldom disobeyed his wife; this time Earl arose slowly and reluctantly took the machine by its pearl handle. Relieved of that responsibility, I gathered up my glass of rum and swilled down a bunch of it. From my point of view I couldn't exactly see the names that Earl had written down, save that his penmanship was so large that not more than a dozen words could be fitted to the page. The ink was black and glossy, and the pigment so coarse that it required great patience before it was accepted by the paper. Or vellum, as it might have been. Ravaged by hate, he was the most estimable and vindictive of men, and had gnawed all the feathers from his quill.

"Working on the Constitution?" I asked.

"Maybe I am and maybe I'm not. I don't come over to

your place and tamper with *your* wife and ask what you're doing, do I?"

I had to think back to the beginning of our friendship and then come forward mentally before I could answer:

"I don't have a wife. And anyway, I'm the last person in the world to molest your wife. Why, she could take off all her clothes and dance around the room and it still wouldn't . . ."

"OK, that's enough. I believe you."

"Howard?" the woman politely inquired.

"Yes?"

"How'd you get to be the leader of our little group? That's what people want to know."

"And you, do *you* want to be the leader?" [Pause.] "See? I thought not."

We left the apartment, Earl and I, and after shooing off the car aficionados, opened up the bonnet. The hoses and tubes and other rubberized parts had actually turned into a rigid sort of business full of faults. And then, too, a squirrel or mayhap a rat had nested there during the cold months and had left a lot of evidence behind.

"You actually drove this thing to Vermont and back?"

"So it would appear."

"But you don't even know how to drive!"

"Oh? I do however know how to use the gizmo. Do you?"

We drove toward Manhattan where Casper lived, a vibrant location with a great deal of litter all around. I knew enough about geography to avoid most of the larger settlements occupied by Hispanics and other blackamoors fetched here to enrich the demographic. Casper lived, if that's the word, in a Dominican neighborhood of fat women and nonplussing homicide rates. I tried to make a decent park but then gave over to Earl when people began yelling at me. Luckily I had a pocketful of silver change with which to distract the children. We hurried, wending our way through a gathering mob of tattooed persons with bamboo slivers piercing their noses. As to why our man had selected this neighborhood . . . It was a mystery.

A spiral staircase with an aged carpet led up three floors to the man's two-room apartment. Three several peepholes had been drilled into the door, a ploy that allowed the renter to preview his visitors at three different levels. We took turns rapping at the door, which is to say until Earl recalled that he had left the gizmo behind. This is what we had come to in our old age.

"Sorry," he said. "Maybe I'd better go get it."

I waited for his return. Realizing that I was under inspection from three different levels, I smoked and hummed and bethought me of my youth when my memory had been good enough for any two men, no matter how old. Came then a voice from beyond the door:

"That you Earl?"

"No."

"Oh." And then: "I'm wondering what that thing is you got there. Looks suspicious to me."

"Oh, for God's sakes. This is *Howard* standing out here! Howard with the gizmo under his arm."

"What happened to Earl?"

"Went to get the gizmo! May I perhaps come in? Possibly?"

"I want to understand. Earl went to get the gizmo, and here is Howard with the gizmo under his arm. And I'm supposed to let you in?"

"Oh, for God's sakes."

We were admitted at last, too soon for the one-legged man to have gathered up the scattered newspapers, the overfull ashtrays, and other evidences of his disorganized life. He was a sloppy man, and his mind was sloppy, too. However, I'm always ready to concede that a person might still be a genius without always being like me.

"I'm returning your car," I said. There was only one chair in the apartment, and it belonged to the cat. "I filled it up with gasoline, too."

"White of you. *I*, certainly, wouldn't have dared drive that thing all the way to Wisconsin and back."

"The gizmo works real well."

"Is that really true Howard? Or is this just another of your . . ."

"No, no, no. Works real well. Ask Earl."

"Can't. He's all out of breath."

We waited for Earl to recover himself. Meanwhile he did make some effort, our host, to hobble off with the ashtray and bring it back in time for me to use it. He had several important pictures on the wall, including the 1941 portrait of Rudolph Hess in full uniform. The most impecunious member of our association, he possessed no more than fifteen (Casper not Hess), or possibly twenty books stacked on top the refrigerator. They were to serve, he had said, to *kick start* (to use an old slave holder's expression), kick start the new civilization we had in mind. Me, I would have placed them on the window sill.

"Got a light?" he asked.

I loaned him my lighter.

"And cigarette? The lighter is useless without it."

At one time his sofa wouldn't have been long enough for me, proving once again that I had lost a good deal of my erstwhile height. Availing myself of that tatty piece of furniture, I slept comfortably for four, possibly five hours, and then awoke to find Earl in bed and Casper sleeping on the floor. No one could have thought our host a handsome man, not with his mouth open, and for an instant I was tempted to use the gizmo on him.

"Casper! Time to wake up," I said.

"Why?"

"Well! We need to get in touch with K."

"Again I ask why."

"Well!"

He lived, K, three doors down and eighty-six blocks away. We found him with a book in one hand and his feet in a tub of water. His habitation was quite ordinary, but did have books in it.

"Come on in! Make yourselves at home!" he averred.

"Don't pay any attention to us. Say, aren't you going to offer us a drink or something? Coffee even?"

"Good ole K! City's preeminent dust aficionado."

The man groaned, but then did finally extricate himself from his footbath and go for coffee. I disliked the disorder in this place, Casper's habits carried to the next higher power. I was tempted to take my kerchief and brush the crumbs off the chair, except that I also disliked being laughed at. If only these were not the best people on earth.

The coffee, too, was poor, and we were made to wait a good ten or fifteen minutes while our host got into his suit, a dark blue double-breasted affair from the 1940s. Nor was he altogether unhandsome himself, except for that perforated nose and a disabling tic that had his left eyebrow forever jumping up and down. His boutonniere was plastic, and his two feet were of such unlike size that he must buy four shoes to assemble one usable pair. As to his capacity for hatred, I was as confident of his as of mine.

"Where're we going?"

"Ask Howard. He's the one who makes the decisions around here."

"Where we going Howard?"

"Me? Oh, I don't know. What do you want to do?"

"What about it, Earl? What do you want to do?"

"I don't know. What about you?"

"Me? I'll do what K wants to do."

"K, yes. Or that adenoidal figure standing just next to him."

I reacted without hesitation: "Really, you oughtn't describe me in that anecdotal fashion. No one should."

I had succeeded in intimidating him. He had spilled coffee down the front of his dickey and was trying to clean it up.

"We could stay here," Casper mooted. "Play poker. Drink."

"No, I can't support that. Place gives me the creeps."

"Hey, I got it! We could go over to the maternity ward. They must have a whole new installation by now."

The Westerfield Maternity Ward was a tax-supported and highly popular facility for the breeding population that allowed open visitation during certain hours. After brief consultation we four, or three of us anyway, settled upon this as the best way to get rid of the afternoon. The gizmo we left behind.

We likewise eschewed the Frasier. The price of gasoline had increased over the past few days, and Casper's insurance had lapsed two days earlier. We sallied forth on foot therefore, trailed by the one-legged man. Still further behind came K, whose huge feet, both of them very soft and inordinately flat, hadn't been designed for traveling on city sidewalks. On the other hand, or foot rather, we were much better able to protect one another when traveling in a line.

We waited a long time for the subway, and when finally it came the cars proved to be freighted with undesirable types. I discerned two times as many trespassers as real Americans, most of them of obvious bad quality.

"Oh, good! Peruvians would you say? Or Hondurans?"

"That's America you're looking at Howard. Our day has come and gone."

"Yes, we were just too successful, don't you see, and have to be punished for it." And then in quiet voice: "Not that even we are what we used to be."

We leapt on board the train and took up positions fore and aft. I could have swept the car with our weapon, had only we brought it, and after about 30 seconds, could had witnessed some very strange facial expressions. I did not however wish to sweep an elderly white woman just across from me, a civilized sort of person holding an old-fashioned handbag in her lap. Yes, and at one time the country had been populated with such people, a disciplined folk who had bequeathed enough and more than enough to provide their offspring with their choice of evils. I locked gazes with a sneering youth with tattooed eyelids, and then an Asian girl of some description with the dead grey eyes of a snake. Impossible not to notice how in recent months American women, fearful of being abducted off the streets and given clitorectomies, seldom ventured abroad without their sons or husbands. Worse still was it that the terrorists, properly so-called, seemed actually to believe in something. Could anything be more dangerous than that? That was when I was pushed aside by a fat man in a T-shirt displaying the emblem of a famous baseball team.

"Pay no attention," Casper recommended, coming to my side. "We have to accept the world in its present configuration."

"No, we don't."

"Or, we could murder a few million of them."

(That good old man! he was always able to dispel my moods. Seeing the success he was having, he went on with it.)

"Kill ten million."

"Right."

"These are not good people Howie."

"I know."

"They have no supernal values. The things they want are all available in shopping malls."

"And yet perhaps some of them . . ."

"No! Just no! Look at those faces."

The faces were frightful, and yet looked all alike. Of those teeming youths, I could approve just two. That was when I noticed that K hadn't come with us.

We left the train, we three, at the first opportunity and then hurried up to street level and sought about for a taxi. It was a bad area, the one we had chosen, with but few Caucasians. And even these were mostly bad.

"Look at that one," said Earl, indicating an obvious alcoholic with whiskers and unbuttoned pants. "He's weak."

"Yes, I suppose. But we don't know what he's endured. The temptations he's had to face."

"Temptations? Temptations? No one ever had as many temptations as me!"

"Oh? And just what were those Earl?"

"Just because I can't remember, that doesn't mean I didn't have 'em!"

He was the youngest of us, and still had time for additional problems and temptations. *He'd* have no reluctance putting the gizmo to work. Came then a taxicab, the driver swerving off at the last moment. Afternoon was drawing on, and we were no nearer to the maternity ward than of an hour earlier.

"Hey! I thought we were going to take the subway."

"We did. We took it, and then we got off again."

"How come?"

"Because we have to go back for K!"

"Ah. Well if that's what the majority wants."

"Am I the only one actively seeking for a cab?"

"One is all we need. Shithead."

"Say, that looks like K right over there!"

"In the yellow pants?"

"Right."

"Well, let me ask you this—is K a negro?"

"No."

"And is that person over there not a negro? And may I

ask why you're holding on to your dick like that?"

"Hurts."

"We *all* hurt Casp. It's part of the times. I probably hurt more than anyone here."

"Oh, yes? I seriously doubt that Howie."

That was when a third taxi driver perceived us and actually came forward. He seemed to be an East European Balt of some description, reckoning by his head's stubborn shape and his deleterious accent. We waited for him to thrust open the door for us. There was a peculiar odor in the vehicle together with certain foodstuffs on the floor. But when the question came up, none of us could properly describe where we wished to go.

"Two stops further on," Earl submitted. "No, wait! Maybe not."

"Oh, good," said the driver. "I should have known."

"Come on, let's get on with it for Christ's sakes! Earl's not going to wait all day."

"I'm Earl."

"I'll look out this window if you fellows will look out that one."

"This window, as you call it, is actually just a piece of cardboard. And opaque."

(It formed a mirror, that pane of glass, giving me yet another unwanted reflection of myself. I was beginning to look like a dignitary of sorts, maybe a waiter in a superior restaurant, an usher or mortician, or like a retired man in the back of a taxicab.)

"You know, I'm getting just a little bit tired of all this. Why don't we forget the maternity part and just go to the movies? Besides, I need to go to the restroom."

"Restroom again? You're sick."

I bent forward—someone had to do it—and gave the driver the hospital address, a piece of information that caused him suddenly to turn in a circle and run off in the other direction. Very soon we were in one of the city's most crowded venues, a maelstrom of second-and third-rate pedestrians trying to work their way past each other. Nor was the driver an especially admirable sort; his head was poorly shaped and looked like a wad of some kind.

"How much further," I asked, "to the hospital?"

"You can get out now if you want to. I won't even charge you nothing."

"In other words you would charge us *something*, yes?"

"Huh?"

"Double negative."

He came to a stop. I had only wanted to amuse my colleagues.

The hospital was a four-story affair with a Salvadorian flag furling from the mast. We strode successfully past the guard, a Mestizo with dental problems and the tattoo of a hat on his otherwise bald head. The elevator had three persons in it wearing serious faces, an improvement over the general run of those we had seen this day. A woman was weeping, a tiny bird was flitting back and forth, and the operator was talking to herself. Regarding this third person I said "Now *there's* a brave one. Her beauty is three-fourths gone, but she's still hanging on to the little bit that remains. Trying to fulfill her mission!"

"Her mission?"

"To love, and inspire it in others."

"She can't hear you—is that what you think?"

The ward was less crowded than usual, and a whole new population of new-born babies had been put on display. My attention was mostly for a tiny and probably premature infant with a beet-red face, a living embarrassment for those as had spawned the thing. Not that the others were a great deal better, judging from their facial expressions, their noises and self-presentation. This then was the future of America, a taxonomic horror more heterogeneous than a gift box of assorted chocolates. Naturally we tended to gather about the most wide-awake and percipient-looking of the lot, a Caucasian product deep in thought.

"Yes, that's the best of them," said K, who had arrived a good deal earlier than us and had nearly finished a serving of coffee contained in one of those abominable white Styrofoam cups without a handle. "A scientist to be sure."

"Possibly. But what sort of scientist? An actual scientist, or someone like Earl?"

"A paleontologist."

"By Jove, you may be right."

"Of course I'm right! Or classicist."

"He might be a classicist, or he might not. At any event he's wise enough to keep his eyes shut as long as possible in this new world."

"OK, let's give this one an "eight" on our ten-scale. Now what about this little fellow?"

"'Fellow'? That's a *girl*, you blockhead!"

We moved three spaces down to where a Spanish or Italian or conceivably a Greek child lay in an accretion of his own personal wastes.

"And yet he doesn't drool as much as the others. And then, too, one must suppose that at least his mother loves him."

"Oh, I see—we're starting with the best, and then going downhill. OK, I'm willing to give this one a 'five,' or maybe a 'six' on our scale. Write it down Casper."

"Jolly well tired of writing things down!"

"Is? And yet you've already agreed to do our group biography, if I remember rightly."

He groaned and looked to heaven, but then did actually take the pencil and begin to fill the sheet with the rankings and quick sketches of the children. Unable to get a clear view inside the ward's incubator, he drew an imagined portrait of the inhabitant's face and gave it a rating, too. We made no attempt to evaluate the parts and pieces of a disaggregated fetus that lay in a bassinet with pink ribbon.

"Should we go on with this?" K courteously inquired. "We're getting into the dregs now. Oh, oh, look at that one. The police are going to have a lot of trouble with him."

Even so, we continued for a short while, saying nothing when we came to a spate of stunned-looking infants waving their arms about. Visitors had come and gone, leaving toys and food stamps for the newly born. Nor made we any remark when we arrived at someone's offspring seemingly lost in the delirium of her mother's cocaine. That was when the supervisor came up, a severe-looking woman wearing military decorations on her kepi and breast.

"We close at five."

"Give you fifty bucks for that blond-headed squirt down at the end," said K, bring his characteristic humor into play.

We drifted down to the emergency room and waited off to one side as an ambulance was being unloaded. The lucky one was dead, the others so mutilated they looked like illustrations in a medical text providing cut-away views of the human midsection.

"In cases like this," said K, "I'm inclined to think of that bad day at Adrianople in ------- with corpses scattered all about."

"And your own corpse? Won't be long before all four of us are stretched out exactly where these poor sons-of-bitches . . ."

"Morbid, K. And you always have been."

"Ha! And so *that's* what it looks like. Notice how the intestine has actually broken open, emitting excrement all about."

We turned and went away. No longer did we visit the cancer ward on any routine basis, not since two of us had also been diagnosed with that disease. We moved past an ancient woman standing quite naked in her open door, and then an earnest-looking little nurse carrying an overflowing bedpan, her place in paradise assured.

We reassembled, all save K, at the intersection of George Fourth and some other street and then dawdled for a time in front of a boutique that specialized in rubber and leather products for adults. Was it time for us to have another cup of coffee? No, not 'less we wanted to halt every few minutes for our most fluent member to visit one of the two public restrooms still available in New York City. Instead we chose to amble on down to MLK and Martin Luther King where some dozen of the unemployed had formed up in front of a movie theatre. Of we four, not one of us had patronized any such place in years. Myself, I preferred those old western films portraying a bleak topography full of a tiny number of short-tempered people engaged in moral disagreements.

"I used to like a good film now and again," said Casper wistfully. "But I got tired of all those naked people all the time. Is that supposed to be exciting or something?"

"Can't make a profit without it. Last time I saw one of these things they had two fuck scenes and a blowjob."

"Well, tell me Earl, could you see the semen spilling out of the girl's mouth? Must have been entrancing. Do make me a list, would you, of the country's preeminent film producers?"

"I seem to remember when films were good as books, or nearly. And then, they used to have these girls don't you know. Sweet ones. Dead now, I suppose."

"I would of married Gail Russell. But she never asked me."

"Ann Blyth. You could take today's sluts and mash 'em up together, they still wouldn't be as pretty as Ann Blyth."

"She was pretty enough. But if you want a woman with *soul*, sooner or later you'll have to marry Gail Russell."

"A lovely woman is a work of art, and they're right, those types, to spend ten hours a day burnishing themselves."

But by this time people were exiting the theatre, giving us the opportunity to evaluate this more or less representative sample of today's American people.

K was waiting for us in a new-style coffee shop with three different restrooms for the country's three main kinds of people. An impatient man, he was having a bad time trying to choose between the thirty or forty coffees on sale, some of them more roasted than others, others more toasted. Nothing was personally more irritating to him (and to me), than persons of this kind, the sort as would prefer to starve than cut into a steak that was just medium instead of well-done. He didn't say anything however.

There were other people in that shop, including one with a face that appeared somewhat more evolved than the generality of them. We looked at each other, or at least until my superior concentration forced his eyebeams off to one side. It was no good, him suddenly pretending to be engrossed in the menu. Not that he was hopeless; give me ten percent of him, thirty-five percent of the woman in the corner, twelve percent of our dutiful waiter, and the rest of me and I could have fabricated a whole new civilization. Suddenly I turned and looked behind me. The walls of that shop were of concrete and a bullet coming in my direction would have to pass through at least two of my colleagues before impinging on me.

"You talk Howie, but we still don't know much about your theories. Or why we've handed the fate of the world over to you."

"Me? Capeheart has the gizmo."

"Capeheart? Casper you mean?"

"Your theories Howard—the time has come to reveal them."

The coffee was good, pretty good, but by no means worth the tariff. I had seen better stuff in Tegucigalpa, the home of one of my woman friends.

"Theories, Howard."

"Well!" I stood. "All I have ever wanted is an advanced society with impossible standards. A crystalline world governed by aesthetes. A tiny group of unforgiving geniuses."

"Howie! You just *must* run for election. The voters would love it."

"A place where integrity has precedence over everything."

They laughed, some of them.

"Have you ever actually known anyone with integrity? In New York City I mean?"

"Someday," I went on, "our cites shall all be made of green marble. People will live in towers scaled to the quality of the inhabitants. Great music fills the air. We shall breed indigo buntings and tropical butterflies."

Charmed by my prophecy, two of the other customers had turned their chairs in my direction. Encouraged by that, I went on to describe my theory of value as a function of:

1) Literary novelists

2) Philosophers, poets, cosmologists, cosmetologists

(The above-listed, and them alone, are authorized to wear the purple.)

3) Soldiers

4) Proctologists

5) Orchestra conductors, reactionary docents, goldsmiths, engravers, stone masons

6) Police

7) Chemists

8) Farmers

9) Carpenters

10) Hypnotists

11) Potters

12) Executioners

13) Ranchers, fishermen

14) Bookbinders, stain glass compositors, organ build-
ers

15) Interrogators

16) Philatelists

And so forth and so on, all the way down to:

2012) Advertisers

2013) Public Relations

2014) Male Prostitutes

2015) Television producers

2017) Cannibals, homosexuals, rapists, lobbyists

and then finally

2018) SPLC members

"Well all right!" Casper said. "We were right to take you as our leader. Except for that business about potters. Little old women, most of 'em."

That was when Earl, picking up the thread of a story that had nothing to do with the present conversation, be-gan narrating in his dreamy way:

"Seems like my grandfather needed linseed oil for some reason or another, and the smell of that stuff, not a bad smell really, still infests the whole property. I can't walk in the front door without being reminded of those days. It has to do, I feel sure, with the proximity of the scent and memory organs inside the human brain," etc.

We looked at him. By this time the management and many of our nearest fellow customers had turned away and wanted us to leave. As the wealthiest of our crowd, I paid for my own coffee and then escorted the others to the door. The streets were running over with New York-ers, their thoughts riveted on money concerns.

K had left us, and no doubt was a hundred yards fur-ther down the road. He could not have known that we would stumble upon one of the new "cigar divans," a nar-row establishment squeezed in between two warring sun-tan salons.

Despising cigars, I chose the least expensive one on offer, a Panamanian product about ten inches long, and
then went to a clean-looking pallet near the rear of the
shop. Earl and Casper followed, but needed the help of the
serving girl to ignite what in one case was an inexpensive
stogie of Indonesian leaf, and in the other a black item
that looked as if it were composed of licorice. Somehow K
had arrived there before us.

"Draw slowly upon these beauties," he said, "and let the
smoke filtrate slowly through thine lungs!"

"This place have a restroom?"

"Look at that. Son-of-bitch" (Casper) "has fallen to
sleep already!"

We smoked. I hadn't had a serious headache in ages,
an accomplishment that was about to be broken. And yet
. . . And yet . . ."

It seemed to me that I was hearing a selection from
Mahler's *Eighth*, there where the children's choir makes
an entrance. For one blessed moment I thought I might
actually be ascending to paradise, which is to say until I
recognized that one of the serving women had put that
particular recording on the machine. Even so, the ambi-
ance was superb, and the other smokers, decently-
dressed, most of them, had the look of educated persons.

"Good to see you again," said the nearest man, a mature individual whom I couldn't recall having ever seen
before. "Interesting crew, these friends of yours."

"Thank you."

"We know about that machine of course."

I nearly fainted. "Machine?"

"As you wish. We don't have to talk about that if you
don't want to. These days I'm more involved with gamma
probes. Parallel universes"—he laughed—"and that sort of
thing."

"One could do worse than parallel universes."

"However, I'm feeling just a little bit drowsy at this

moment, and so I think I'm going to turn over—I'm doing it now—and face in the other direction. Cigar is making me sick."

In the end, we wasted more time there than was beneficial for any of us. On the other hand Earl had located the restroom and was disinclined to leave it. Having finally returned to us, he took up his former position and began speaking in his far-away voice:

"Lawrence, the desert Lawrence, tells of the great troubles he had finding watering holes in the sand. That's the way with me and restrooms in this blistered town."

"Indeed. But he" (Lawrence) "was trying to *acquire* water, not dispense it."

"You're a trivial man Howie, and always will be."

"He knows about the gizmo," said I as quietly as possible, nodding toward that fifth person eavesdropping from his divan.

"What!"

"Put him on the list! We'll take care of him as soon as we've finished with the Hollywood people."

I wrote it down, a difficult project in all that dim. That was when a policeman entered and after examining everyone's papers, turned and went out again.

Fifteen

I needed three days to recover from the smoke. And then on Monday I awoke a little too early and after hesitating for about an hour—life requires courage—got slowly but completely out of bed. Right away I saw that my alpha chameleon, the one that had been missing for a week, had come back home again. He had had some adventures, no doubt about that, but at the end of the day had opted for a more settled manner of life.

They formed a tumultuous crowd, my chameleons. I happened to be in process of feeding the scoundrels when just then I heard someone tampering uselessly with the foolproof locks at my apartment door. Responding to the noise, the escrubilator (wrapped in blue paper) was quickly thrust upon me from the hand of an obvious mestizo with a nasty smile and repellent moustache. I gave the fellow a coin but had to wait a long time for the change. My mind fell back to Chairman *Reuben Pefley*, who had promised to free the country of all such people. How was I know that in times to come that commitment would finally once and for all be consummated? I couldn't then, but do so now.

Casper had enclosed a note. In his youth the genius had passed full eighteen months at L'Ecole Nationale des Chartes in Paris, France, and the quality of his penmanship had "run off the tracks," as K was wont to say. The man wrote from right to left and no longer bothered with several other Western traditions. But I was able to get the gist of it.

He had used the gizmo on a cat. He was no longer willing to be responsible for the instrument's safekeeping. He had been visited by three unsmiling men dressed in dark suits and high cost wristwatches. Additionally, they carried laminated identity cards with federal totems on them. But by great good hap, he (Casper) had already deposited the device with a vibrant woman—she would do anything for money—who lived two floors beneath him. And now the goddamn thing was being returned to me.

Sixteen

And so it fell out that in the fullness of time we collected at our favorite meeting place and after wheedling the tavern keeper for the backroom key, at last set about discussing our prospects in real seriousness. K, it is true, was going through an episode of endocrinal problems and wasn't expected actually to speak. As always the group relied upon their leader to inaugurate the conversation.

"My recommendation is that . . ."

"Shut up Howard. Earl has something to say."

Instead, it was Casper who spoke: "*My* recommendation is that we just lay low for a few weeks. Or months."

"Oh, good. I been laying low for *seventy-eight years!*"

"And K agrees."

"Is that because he can't speak?"

(It's a hard thing to witness geniuses in conflict. And then, too, we hadn't realized that the room wasn't fully empty.)

"You don't usually dispose of malefactors just by lying low," Earl asserted, speaking loud and clear. "But tell me if I'm wrong."

K just then began coughing, and as so often before, managed to come up with a wad of blue-green phlegm which came to land in one of the worst locations. It was incumbent upon me to keep the conversation going.

"Gentlemen! We've worked so hard and for so long, maybe we deserve a short vacation before continuing on."

"Vacation! Myself, I've always wanted to see Iceland. Volcanoes and whatnot."

"Wouldn't advise it," came a voice from the far corner. The man's face was fully invisible in the insufficient light. "Been there, done that."

"Ecuador perhaps?"

"Shut up Howard. You know, some of us are getting just a little bit tired of that condescending tone of yours. Always having to hear about that little four-point IQ advantage of yours. After all, the three of us have 457 points, collectively speaking."

I hushed. Better to allow them to muddle about for an hour or two before personally intervening. Suddenly K spoke up in a wheezy voice accompanied by hand movements.

"You people! Some of us are going to be dead before

we've killed anybody!"

"He's right. Hell, we might all be dead by then. Howard's half-dead already."

I ignored it, the price of leadership among high grade people. That was when the bartender entered, looked us over, and went out again. No one seeing us from a distance of, say, thirty feet or more, could have imagined we were the most dangerous association on earth.

"Tell about the cat."

"The cat. She was a big one alright. Noisy. Her fur, if any, was exiguous, and of course her pupils dilated vertically instead of like a person's. You will have seen that same uncanny trait in the pictures of certain kinds of alligators. It didn't bother me at all to close the book on her."

"You buried her?"

"Bury? You just don't seem to understand do you? I'd of had to pick her up in a dustpan for goodness sakes! Ask Howard."

"Howard's not speaking."

"Nothing but broken atoms lying about."

"Blimey. We need more of these things."

"More? And you not willing to use the one we've already got?"

Finally, with the sun deteriorating in the west, the rabble in the next room growing ever noisier—(I craved to slay the lot of them)—and the music proving more and more barbaric, I gave myself the floor:

"The gizmo shall certainly be put into use at the time appropriate for that."

"And when might that be Howard?"

"When we've agreed upon the targets. For example, I haven't the least idea whom Earl wishes to granulate."

Earl stood up. His philosophy seemed to have gelled during the last few weeks. "Everybody, Howard. Everybody in the coastal regions. Have you never thought what our country might still be if only California were rendered vacant? Or left with nothing except maybe some of those real big trees?"

"California? California isn't nearly as iniquitous as Massachusetts."

"Look, we don't have to restrict ourselves to just one state. Or just one country neither."

I wrote both states down, recognizing as I did so that we might improvidently destroy a half-dozen or so good persons in the process. As if he were in contact with my thinking, K asked:

"What about the good people?"

"Again with that? This is *California* we're talking about! A people with that climate and that acreage ought to have built a real civilization by now."

No disagreement came to my ears. Taking up my pad and pencil I underlined the word in red ink.

"Good! What about you Casp? Whom do you want to discontinue?"

He stood. "Truth is, Howard, it's a little more complicated in my case."

"Tell us."

"It would require giving everyone a battery of tests."

"You want to kill off all the stupid people? That's really harsh Casp."

"Not at all. No, no, no. I just want to make some sort of dispositive arrangement for gifted people who act like mediocrities. People who could have achieved something but didn't want to bother."

His testimony was received in silence, which is to say until Earl stood again and spoke out loud and clear in his well-intentioned way. "No doubt. But you must remember that exceptionality is frowned upon in this system. It makes everyone else feel bad. Such people generally end up as heroin addicts."

"Then let us eliminate the democracy!"

"My dear friend, the democracy is eliminating itself at

breathtaking speed. I thought you knew."

"Shouldn't we ask K's opinion?"

"Oh, I don't think that's necessary."

Earl stood up again. "You want the best possible world? Then I assume you want the best people. Tell me, I beg you, the last time a non-Caucasian race proved able to set up and sustain a high culture?"

"Japanese?"

"Possibly. And so we'll allow them to live."

"Chinks?"

"The jury is still out on that one. Anyone else?"

"But just look at the Chinese alph . . . Ha! I had started to call it an 'alphabet.' Harder than Cherokee it is!"

"Yes. A wise people would have phoneticized that mess by now. Let's leave those people to themselves shall we? '*Let China sleep,*' someone said."

"But they aren't. Sleeping."

I was trying to write this down. With all of us now standing, the adventitious person in the corner had begun laughing out loud at our deliberations. A perfect candidate for our first human trial, had only I brought the gizmo with me.

He had never been the bravest of us, Casper had not, not since he had lost a leg and eye. Terrified equally of the subway and the Brooklyn streets, I offered to accompany him as far as the Kurtagić Building, beyond which point the danger was "exponential," as I tried to explain.

"And yet you claim to be so brave," he averred.

"I'm *fairly* brave. About a seven on my personal ten-scale. Except for that, I have no fear at all."

"Sure! Not so long as you got that big ole gun with you all the time."

I stopped. "Who told you about that?"

"I can see it! The goddamn barrel is sticking out!"

By this time we had covered a full block and had

passed into a broken-down residential district near the exact center of the borough. Here the families had retired into their locked and bolted cells and were huddling for warmth around their high-resolution television sets. Glancing skyward I detected a human head protruding from one of the upper windows, though I did manage to skip out of range before her sputum hit the ground. What did they want, these people, and why had they chosen to reside in such propinquity, one to another? And why had I?

The sea was near. We sniffed at it, Casp and I, both of us aware of the rising waters that had already wrought such a lot of troubles at Sheep's Head Bay.

"We'll never see it," said I. "The day salt water reaches the twentieth floor of that somewhat unsteady structure over there."

"The black one?"

"Nay, nay, that grey structure squeezed in between the tall one and the wee one to the latter's immediate right."

"Good Lord Howard, the wee one and the latter one have got to be the same! Besides, that thing doesn't even got twenty stories."

"The devil you say."

We counted. In fact there *were* twenty stories, even if just barely.

"See?"

"Yes, yes. You're a scholar Howie. Everybody knows that."

"So hand over the twenty dollars."

"Say what?"

"Twenty dollars. It *was* a fair bet after all."

"I don't remember any such bet as that!"

"You're getting old Casp, and I'm really beginning to worry about that memory of yours. Bodes ill, that does."

He paid. I was already carrying better than a hundred dollars in bills and coin and another fifteen or thereabouts in subway tokens. My guess was that in order to pay his rent, the poor man would be needing that twenty-dollar bill. "How poor are you Casp? No, I mean really?"

"Damn poor. But not poor enough to swindle my friends. And you, how rich are you?"

I cited my assets, giving prominence to the approximately seventeen thousand bequeathed me by an uncle, a naive man who had believed himself to be in general agreement with my theories. Next I described my pension, subtracting the portion donated to a certain nativist organization. I described my book royalties, the proceeds from my two patents, my furniture and surviving Chameleons, my electronic devices and the free rent that came from serving as arbiter of the conflicts that very often emerged between the tenants. And in short, having explained it all, my friend could see that I was nearly as poor as he.

"Gosh. I always thought you were so rich."

"No, no; that's *arrogance* you see, not money."

"Well I'll be jiggered. Even so, I think you ought to share with me. Another year or two and we'll both be dead anyway."

That was true.

We continued into the awful night. The smell of the sea had abandoned us, giving way to the mystic scents of rotting garbage and respirating asphalt. We met an ancient woman with a cat in her arms, a blind man (this one genuine), who hadn't been told that it was night, and then a large policeman sheltering beneath the awning of the abandoned Sea Merchants headquarters. It was here that the confused and nostalgic Casper began to speak of his dismay at the modern age.

"It just gets worse and worse. What happened Howard?"

"I have my theories about that."

"Sure would like to hear what they are."

I made no immediate reply. The night weighed upon us, and reminded me of dreams endured during my psychotic period, when I seemed to be standing face to face with millions of average people who hated my very existence. Meantime the actual city was deteriorating in front of my eyes, a worrying sight that allotted us glimpses of dangerous individuals standing here and there on street corners meditating acts of violence.

"My theory," said I, returning to that, "has to do with too much prosperity too far prolonged. Humans can endure only just so much of that before they start to rot."

"I'm not seeing a lot of prosperity Howard. Not hereabouts anyhow."

"It dissolves self-discipline, and lets people do all sorts of things they oughtn't. But the real problem is this, how capitalism has such a disparate impact on good people. Quantity over quality. Bad people lording it over the good. I intend to kill every last one of them."

"You're getting mad just talking about it. Aren't you?"

"Little bit. I was hardly out of my youth before I saw that history proceeds, not in cycles, far less dialectically or like a pinball machine, but like a kaleidoscope with great chunks of pure horror falling suddenly in place."

"Whew! You're so smart Howie."

I always dismiss that sort of flattery.

"In what ways am I particularly so smart?"

"Or maybe you're just one of those people who hates to see anyone having fun."

"Fun? All that grunting and laughing? Jumping up and down and making odd faces? I may not be as old as you Casper, but I can remember when boys and girls had turned into adults by age of sixteen."

"And you'd like to bring that back wouldn't you? A poor economy, everyone with their noses to the grindstone? A dangerous world?"

"I would. Life without danger . . ."

". . . isn't worth living.'"

Obviously we had read the same books. Just then a car passed by, slowed, and then turned and came back. In the lamplight I could see the profiles of three egg-shaped heads.

"Something thrilling this way comes. That there gun of yours is loaded I assume."

"Henceforward, I carry the gizmo everywhere I go."

We reached Casper's wretched quarters at just past eleven. No one had meddled with the drop of glycerin (a more cohesive agent than water), deposited carefully on top the doorknob, and we were able to enter the place in safety. His books were few but of the best quality our civilization has yet produced. His computer, on the other hand, was broken, as could be seen in the number of parts lying at random here and there. He had just two pictures on the wall, an etching of the young James Earl Ray and a schedule of high tides forecast for New York Harbor. We drank whiskey. During our discussion, I had let myself become more excited than I should, wherefore I decided to take up a more calm and equitable frame of mind.

"When I hear the word 'progress,' that's when I draw my gizmo."

"Right. No such thing as progress. So why are we killing all these people?"

"Because!" (I did try to remain calm.) "Remember this, that the eradication of America was no doubt implicit in its egalitarian origins, but the on-going decay of Europe is a monstrous thing."

"The scoundrels. I'll add 'em to the list."

Seventeen

With every day that passed, the future grew that much

nearer. My own tenure on earth, such as it had been, was also passing, and on June 23rd I volunteered to spend the entire day lying in bed.

First, I went hurriedly through a succession of two-minute dreams, each offering a personal vision of hell and/or heaven. To start, I conceived of a bright sunny day where hysteric bees and dragonflies went about servicing the flowers. And in the distance, a bright blue river with quicksilver splotches riding on the current. Instructed by the dog, I stepped through a maze of brown stubble down to where rollicking pumpkins, greedy for summer, infested the field. I harkened to the cautionary sound of iron bells emanating from the city.

I awoke, consulted the clock, and then began to imagine that I was in a nineteenth-century city. It must have been a Sunday, judging from the dress and dignity of tall silent men moving in a circuit about the courthouse square. You must remember how in those days the farms and towns were wont to overlap one another, offering views, for example, of virgins reading books of poetry in their gazebos. The smells then were mainly of warehoused products—cotton, soybeans, and seasoned hay, the best of all smells apart from the usual magnolia, honeysuckle, gardenia, and biscuits baking in the oven. Ended here the first and second of those dreams.

Having leveraged myself out of bed, I disabled my telephone, shut down the escrubilator, and made a quick inventory of the K–N range of my library. I have never denied my fixation on the beauties and the information to be had from books, nor my refusal to have any sort of dealings with those who didn't feel the same. Suddenly I drew out an eighteenth-century tome in unreadable German (the binding in awful condition) and allowed the thing to open where it would. The text, as explained, was unreadable, and happened to have been composed in a language of which I was overwhelmingly ignorant. However (and this was the main thing), someone had left behind on page 143 an obscene sketch composed in a black ink already much faded. Joined in laughter, we two, the artist and me, had broken through the two hundred years of water-colored time that was supposed to have prevented us from meeting. Books do that.

My third dream of that day, occurring around 9:15 or 9:30, was a more complicated business and featured a larger cast than the previous ones. Unfortunately I remember nothing about it. Instead I shaved and rested and then took down the gizmo (I had started to call it the "gazebo") and lubricated the "mouth parts" (we called them) with a thin application of eucalyptus oil. Already the thing had used up more than two percent of its programmed longevity, and so far we had accomplished nothing. Except this—that it really did give a person an exquisite feeling, knowing that though he might be old and basically defunct yet was he also in possession of a miracle weapon capable of ionizing any malefactor to come within a thousand miles. Suddenly, on an unwise compulsion, I entered the code, launched the fuse, aimed, and burned a six-inch hole in the wall between my bedroom and kitchen.

I spent the afternoon trying to read, a project that had become more difficult as my mind, becoming always smaller, had grown congested with little fragments of heterogeneous information of every sort. I wasted an hour on a piece of academic garbage and then another few minutes scanning a medieval Hungarian history known neither to the Bibliothèque Nationale nor The Library of Congress. It was good preparation, this last-mentioned, for the dream-state that awaited me:

I dreamt that I had been transported to a place where the connection between wealth and fame on the one part and genius and good behavior on the other had finally and forever been severed. A place where all attention was focused on the small things, on finance and gold futures, gas mileage, politics, and basketball. I envisioned people walking about with nose rings and tattoos on their persons. Entrapped in this place, I squirmed and called and beat my head against the dream-state wall. Worse was to realize that although I had been dreaming, I hadn't been sleeping.

When I was young, I had tried to extinguish the sun by Will alone. Having failed at that, I now brought into play what remained of that effort and used it to extricate myself from this nightmare of three o'clock in the afternoon. I had almost exhausted my stockpile of wines and rums, but managed all the same to put together a mixed drink of a potency sufficient to the need. That was when K began pounding on my door at the precise same time as I began ignoring him.

Eighteen

I had one further dream that day, an extended delusion in which K had returned to my door and was fuddling with the lock. It was nothing but a dream of course, while the true K was actually going through a series of his own reveries on the other side of town.

Later on we learned that he had betaken himself to the county library, a well-organized public institution named after John Bell Hood. Richly endowed with texts of every sort, the upper level reading room supplied our group with all the materials needed for our research. And yet, after two hours of this, K had understandably begun to grow drowsy and by early afternoon had actually fallen off to sleep amid his books and dictionaries. But here was the main thing: he also began to dream.

He thought at first that he was standing atop an immensely tall building lashed by strong winds. Far below, thousands of New Yorkers had gathered and were throwing stones at him. Years went by.

Secondly, he believed that he was sharing a reading table with persons whose gizmos were more advanced than
his own. He groaned. There were five, perhaps six New
Yorkers sharing his table, "low-hanging fruits," he called
them, all of them grinning back with the mix of contempt
and delight that defined the nature of that city. Even so,
he managed to get back to sleep quickly enough and return to his perch on top the Trayvon Building.

He continued in this state until just past 3:17, whereupon he retired to the men's convenience and locked himself in his accustomed cell. Here, reading more or less ef-
fectively with three volumes balanced in his lap, he again
fell off into an especially uncomfortable slumber that
ought have precluded dreaming. Instead he began to believe that he was granulating people with the gizmo, thousands of them lined up cooperatively in a vacant field.
They who had been humans, now they were tiny little
mounds of sand blowing off in the breeze. He danced on
the heath. Such an improved world it portended! A new
kind of people delivered from the horrors of humanism,
democracy, equality, and all the other obstructions to
human improvement.

He walked home through the crepuscule. The city
lights had summoned all the world's insects, and these in
turn had drawn the bats. Refusing to come too near these
horrors, he paced ahead purposefully, his left paw full of
the handle of a precision-made German knife with a forest
scene graven on the blade. Suddenly he drew the weapon
and flourished it, rehearsing for the time when he might
need it. There was an appreciable number of derelicts in
this area, and even the respectable-looking ones might be
using disguises.

He was too old to be outside in the perilous black night
when he might just as easily have been looking at it
through the peephole in his stain glass window. He could
remember when he was never afraid of anything. Just then

he picked up the scent of a late-night bakery. The city was an awful place, but he did give it credit for this.

He entered, evaluated the two customers, and then immediately came back out again. He hungered for a cup of coffee and a cigarette, but could not right away recall which of these had been made illegal. He yearned for more comfortable shoes, for an end to coughing, for surcease of pain from an old abdominal wound so bravely endured, and for the capacity to conjugate with either of the two lovely girls marching in his direction.

Finally, having done quite enough wandering and dreaming for a full week, he approached Howard's quarters and worked his way to the third story. Here there lived a man who cared so little for the law that he never went out of his way to violate it, and who would cheerfully supply him with coffee, cigarettes, and alcoholic drink. He might be given a pallet to lie on, access to a considerable (if somewhat unusual) collection of books, dozens of versions of Wagner and Mahler, a pretty good view of the night, and a few other things he couldn't just then recall to mind. Therefore he knocked twice, waited, knocked again, and then turned away sadly and directed himself toward his own designated quarters.

Nineteen

Casper's place was not awfully far from a world-famous bridge often seen in paintings and photographs. Reputed to be a superior locality, it was in fact quite the other way around. Asked what was wrong with it, he described a class of prosperous people who had joined the right fraternity while studying what was economically most propitious at the time. One could not set foot in that purlieu without colliding into some of the most adorable little candle and wine shops, a gardening center presided over by a woman in a bonnet, an outlet for collectible comic books, environmental jewelry, and the like. He used to run home past all this, hiding his face from the advanced people and their deodorized dogs. The world had never seen such a healthy demographic, so full of good intentions, tolerant and diverse and as vacuous as outer space. On the other hand, with his eye patch and bamboo crutch, he seldom had to ask anyone to get out of his path.

Oftentimes he used to toddle on down to the wine store and waste a few minutes appraising the labels and curiously shaped bottles. Spent a lot of time, he also did, comparing and contrasting the show windows of the larger department stores. He liked to analyze people, especially at subway stations where large numbers came together from the four corners of the town. Or he might transport himself to one or another of the very popular Euro-coffee shops where instead of sugar (known to cause tooth decay), quaint little pots of brown honey were available. His loathing increased. Had such a health-obsessed people ever before existed? Fools. What, they wanted to live as long as he?

He could go anywhere (anywhere within a seven-block radius), and do all sorts of things not permitted to those with a full set of eyes, legs, and teeth. For example, he might stretch out at full length on his proprietary bench in the nearby park, shield his eye with a newspaper, and even go to sleep for brief periods. All around him the vagrants came and the vagrants went, and the next time he checked, he was a vagrant, too. As for the children, it had needed them only a short time to understand that he never had money with him.

And so thus Casper. He dreamt and while dreaming dreamt that he lived in an America carried to the next higher power, a place in which wealth and human degradation had reciprocally achieved optimal development. Where the best genetic material had been overborne by the worst and where the people adopted without cavil the philosophies recommended on television. Where it was normal for hundreds of millions to rise up all at the same moment and hurry off to where they didn't wish to be. Where love in its newest iteration could just as well be conducted on a three-dimensional printer. Where today's humans looked upon themselves as the best the cosmos had on offer. And where, in short, the principle of democracy had evolved into history's most anodyne and most perfect horror.

Obviously his theories and dreams overlapped, an arrangement of great profit to his red-hot choler. Some days he wanted to demolish the world and all its contents, other times he wished but to punish those who most deserved it, the poor for example, college students, liberals, and the bourgeoisie. He wanted to bear down on cheerful people, on Altaic and Uralic types, on television personalities (them especially), and everyone in the whole wide world who had ever for a moment militated on behalf of progress.

There were more things in his philosophy than dreamt of by earth-bound Americans. His mind ranged among the comets, it reckoned with the pyramids, ran through subway tunnels, visited oriental restaurants. He had so many projects. He could have been an engineer, this man, and might thereby have made life a good deal more convenient for those who hated him. As with landscapes, people were best viewed from a certain remove. He had examined the villages of France, yea and the people, too. Thinking of that, he scurried back to his bench, covered his face with a newspaper, and began calling upon his favorite dream, the most brilliant in his whole inventory, wherein he was traveling forever through a turmoil of bright gorgeous stars.

Twenty

Did I know about these dreams because I had asked? Or because my friends, coming one by one, had wished to tell about them?

"Yes" to the last question and "no" to all the others. Truth is, I knew more about the goings-on of my friends than of particle physics, never my strongest field of study. I saw their frailties in full array, and likewise their admirable qualities, which were many and amazing, and as stalwart as the armies of Epaminondas. Earl was amazing, too, almost in spite of his modest self.

He liked to stay at home almost all the time, and not solely because of his wife. It is of course true that men of genius often suffer from uncomprehending wives. One thinks of Alma Mahler for instance, or Wagner's first wife as compared to his last. None of this was true for Earl's woman, who in the realm of female things was something of a genius, too. Having done a bit of reading, she had chosen to follow in the trajectory of Penelope and Héloïse. She made meals, she flattered her man, she stood guard while he was sleeping. Her lips were cheery, and her bosoms were deep. She even looked after my chameleons when I was out of town.

"Good man, your husband," I once said to her.

"Oh? Doesn't matter to me whether he's good or not."

"Does he speak in his sleep? So that you might know what he is dreaming?"

"Well sure."

"Tell me."

"Absolutely not!"

"It's for his own good."

"Oh. Well last night for example . . ."

"Yes?" I moved closer.

". . . he was talking about 'parallel' things. That was the gist of it."

"Parallel universes?"

"Yes! Something like that. But then he woke up and saw that I was listening."

"OK, never mind about scientific things. But does he ever talk about the future? What's going to happen, and stuff like that?"

She thought. "Well, I know he thinks about the mortgage. And he worries about the duties of being the leader of your little group."

I laughed, but she did not.

"No, no; I mean about 'the end of the world,' and so on. Does he?"

Again she thought. "He talks about you."

"Oh?"

"Yes. But we don't need to get into that."

I gave up. She had just removed a pineapple pie from the oven, and her attention was divided. One could do worse than to sample her cooking while thumbing through one of her husband's esoteric magazines.

Another month had to go by before I could finally get an inkling of Earl's subterraneous thoughts, and on the basis of that form an opinion as to whether he was really the man for what lay in front of us. Was he prepared to explain himself to his generous-minded wife? Adept at driving a getaway car? Ready to turn the gizmo onto himself if such became necessary? It was in pursuance of these concerns that in late August I summoned him to my flat and succeeded in getting him drunk.

"Earl, Earl, Earl," I said. "What makes you behave as you do? Did you have some untoward experiences when you were young?"

"Oh, I see. Just because I'm drunk, you think this is a good time to start asking questions."

"Me? Questions? Is it true that you ran away from home?"

"Yes. But not till I was twenty-seven. And even then I

came back again."

He asked for further wine, and then topped it off with a short nap of somewhere between one and two hours. I was also dozing. Finally, at about 11:15 he came back to life and began revealing more than I cared to know. A projectile fired into my apartment at just that moment would perforce have had to penetrate a decorative pot with a plant in it, next Earl, and then the television before coming to me.

"Most times it was my daddy who used to butcher the hogs," he inserted. "But then he up and died, don't you know."

The man was suffused with nostalgia. We both knew that I was on the verge of asking another question. "What about when you came to New York? And your career, what about that?"

"Career my ass. Never held a job for more than a real short while. These people . . ." (he waved his arm at them) ". . . basically they just work for the money. They can't imagine anything better than that."

"And must be punished, right? These people? So we can bring forth a better sort of man?"

"Naw, I don't care about any better sorts. I just want to kill the ones we got now."

"I'll write that down," I said, taking out my notebook and pencil and as he watched carefully, transcribing his words in big letters. The tablet had six other names in it, people to be spared—a farmer, a plumber, and four pretty girls spotted in restaurants and department stores. "And who will rule over us Earl, once we've deleted the money people? Generals? Ideologues? Priests?"

"How about us four?"

"Earl! We'd be bored to death with that kind of stuff. No, I think we must leave wealth and power in the hands of people who aren't as smart as us."

Twenty-One

Not as smart as us—it left a lot of room. We could entrust the power to a few half-educated souls from off the streets, confident they could not be worse than elected people. This was my remark to Earl, who had gone on drinking throughout the last hour. In the meantime he had taken two telephone calls from his wife, who feared he might have misplaced himself in the enormous city.

He had his quiddities, this Earl, the most unusual of them his ability to summon a series of sequential dreams that carried over from one night to another, the plot getting more and more complicated and the cast more numerous as time went on. He said it was as if he had been living in one of those underground tunnels that vermiculate the New York substrate, only suddenly to push aside the manhole cover and stick his head above the surface. This seemed to be his personal metaphor for the distinction between bad surroundings (the sewer) and what was even worse. We talked about this insight frequently, he and me.

And then on Thursday last, he dreamt that he had been entrusted with the gizmo and with the single sole exception of Abraham Lincoln, had slain more North Americans than anyone in history. He slew them in their apartments, their cars and office buildings, and on July 10th actually did slaughter a pigeon in Alexander Stevens Park, a real achievement in view of the wary nature of those fowl. It oughtn't have surprised him (but did) to find later on that the creature had been fitted with a listening device. That was the day he had been reading, or rereading rather, his favorite part of Guénon in a slim volume published together with a postscript composed by one of that man's most obtuse critics.

By this time it was almost 5:00 in the morning, and with dawn threatening and the alcohol mostly gone, he began, Earl, decanting out loud about still further dreams, an entire anthology of them with reappearing personalities and themes. Of all my friends, this man's dream hoard was far the richest and most abnormal.

"I dreamt," he revealed, "that everyone under the age of seventy was lying face down in the mud. A person could travel for miles by stepping on heads alone."

"Good heavens."

"Dreamt I was aboard a sea-going freighter traveling for eternity through smoke and fog."

"That's better. And the crew, did you have to have dealings with them?"

"No, they knew to keep out of sight."

"Ah. No doubt there was a big library on board that boat. Was it housed, that collection, in your private quarters?"

"It was."

"Leather-bound volumes I presume, with lots of gold tooling?"

"Dern you Howie. And all this time I thought the dream was mine alone."

"Now let's talk about all those port cities you must have been viewing in the black dark night. And other ships, phantoms running abreast mile after mile."

"That, too."

Drinking, we laughed, and laughing, raised high our beakers holding the last of the wine. We had two reasons for wanting to go to Manhattan, and only one of them had novelistic significance.

Long Island Mystery Train! fifteen coaches long. We traveled as far as Wantagh before leaving our places and moving to the forward car in order to avoid the ticket taker. No shortage of drunk people on board, nor vomit neither. We sat across from a woman reading a piece of literary garbage with a risqué cover. Unable to abide it, Earl spoke up loudly in reference to the book, an action that inspired the woman to rise and leave us. By this time we were passing through a series of ghost towns— ------------, -----------, ----------- —now occupied, insofar as they were still occupied at all, by a few score of haunted-looking people waiting on the station platforms.

All of this was bad enough, but not nearly as bad as when middle class people in suits and shoes came aboard with leathern satchels. I focused upon a businessperson of some description who appeared to be going through a postmodern crisis, judging from the spasms in his left eyelid. Bending nearer, I found other less conspicuous disturbances in a man who in more honest times might almost have been a mail carrier for example, or bean farmer, a tinker, or a muleskinner.

By now we were trapped in a crowd of homologous consultants, public relations types, men in suits. I worried about Earl, who seemed on the verge of panic, which is to say until I lifted my cuff to show the .32 caliber Beretta half hidden beneath my sock. Meantime the train continued to gain in speed and altitude, still refusing to stop for dangerous-looking commuters in low-hanging trousers and baseball caps.

We had come a long distance, from there to Penn Station. Putting on my direst expression, I shouldered my way from the train and stepped past the blood pressure machine where I halted, opened my magazine, and began reading of new developments in cryonics. Another machine, one that changed dollars into pesos, was particularly busy. I observed female career women, the most eminently well-dressed group in the world, hurrying past in search of money, titles, promotion, and corner offices.

It required Earl several minutes to disembark. He wanted me to see a brace of African Americans who appeared to be carrying on some sort of sexual endeavor in plain open view. Lest they be convicted of a crime, no one wanted to be caught paying notice to them. We hastened to the business area and after breakfasting on two large cones of cotton candy, rushed through that gigantic lobby to the outside world.

It was certainly New York. Within three minutes a population equal in numbers (though not in quality) to Wyoming's had passed us by on the way to their offices, their domino-shaped buildings, their fur-lined elevators, and light-speed computers, there to remain until they died. And yet I *was* cheered to see at least one normal-looking human, a boy of maybe fifteen years carrying a lunch bag in one hand and an apple in the other. Better he had never lived; six months and either he will have been crushed by the mindset of that place or, worse, will have taken on a New York personality. It reminded me why I had striven so hard and for so long to develop a killing machine.

Two blocks further we found a liquor store squeezed in between an abandoned building and a wholesaler of adult literature. It was a well-supplied sort of place with four security guards and wines from all around the globe. Getting into my glasses, I scanned the labels, a colorful sort of literature showing ships at sea, the pyramids, an old-fashioned cabin in wintertime with smoke coming from the chimney. But mostly I focused upon an Ecuadorian import, hoping that the product was half as good as the scenes of outer space, the finest trademark in the whole establishment. And anyway I was never able to distinguish good wines from bad.

My friend, more drunk than me, had ventured into the dark part of the store, had prized open one of the bottles, and had seated himself on the unclean floor. They hardly noticed, the guards and stereotypical New Yorkers browsing the shelves. "Stereotypical," I say, owing to the lordly facial expressions that came from residing in the nation's most portentous, wealthiest, and most up-to-date city.

Never again, I swore, would I leave home without the gizmo.

I paid for the Ecuadorian wine and then went back for Earl. The son-of-a-bitch had intended to buy a half-dozen bottles of the stuff, including a Romanian product draped with artificial cobwebs to testify how old it was. Of course, needless to say, that was the moment my partner vomited nosily, spraying the left shoe of the superbly-dressed business lady loitering in the vicinity. I wanted to break into applause, but even more than that I wanted to vanish into the crowd. Each of those two shoes had cost two hundred dollars at the least, a price that might have been discounted however when sold as a pair. And where, pray, had my grandmother kept *her* four-hundred-dollar shoes, she who could have thrashed to death this piece of shit with the drawstring of her Sunday bonnet.

I was half-asleep myself and yet managed, by making a detour around the incensed woman, managed to bring Earl outside with just one bottle, the most that he could carry. By good fortune, we managed to hit the street in time to witness several hundred thousand people racing in a panic to their work stations. What is life for after all?

Having marched a full block against the grain of the pedestrians, we turned and moved with the flow. In that great crowd we could have been interlopers from the Cenozoic Era and no one would have noticed. Anonymity! there were perhaps a hundred thousand eyes in that one block, and yet no New Yorker seemed aware of any other. Strange! I recollected how in my southern days I could go downtown with my dog and find six or seven friends in an equal number of minutes. Hell, I could go into the drugstore and borrow a quarter from the proprietor. Or, I could run in any direction and find myself in open country within just minutes. Therefore never ask me again why I abominate big cities.

He vomited again, my friend, but managed this time to

have reached the sewer. Already his bottle was half-empty. Meantime I could plainly hear his wife on the mobile phone, the third time that morning I had heard it. Unaware of her voice, Earl said this:

"Howie?"

"Yes?"

"I want" [insert here the name of his wife] "to have my percentage" (her name was Gwen), "of the gizmo."

"Say what?"

"When I die! We all die, Howard. Sooner or later."

"That's the tradition certainly."

"And I want" [wife again] "to have my share of the royalties."

"Royalties. They're going to pay us royalties for murdering half the population?"

"But which half Howie? That's the nub of it. Which half? Can I have some of your wine."

"No you can't have any more wine!"

"I don't want her to have to go back to work again Howie. She's suffered enough."

"I'll take care of that. Trust me."

We crossed at the intersection, a confusing maneuver that caused me to collide into a young man of considerable size. It infuriates me, the way mature people are treated in this society.

"Goddamn it! Blackguard! By the time I was your age I was reading Thucydides in the original!"

"Xenophon I might believe. Anyway it was your own fault."

"I know that! What, is this some sort of *situational* ethics we got going here?"

Suddenly I lashed out at the fellow, an involuntary thing that situated my left paw aside his right cheek. Beneath my blow I was aware of the man's dentition, which however remained intact. We both suspended operations while he probed his teeth with a hand that had two rings on it. The time had come for us to leave the intersection, an imperative operation that left us glaring at each other in the middle of the street.

"You hit me in the goddamn face!"

"You noticed. And I'll tell you something else, too, and that is that . . ."

"Something else? You haven't told me the first thing yet!"

"I most certainly did! Thucydides!"

"Oh, yeah."

"No, this is my last warning. We will *take you apart*, if it comes to that!"

"'We'?"

I pointed to Earl, a sorry figure crumpled up against the First Monetized Bank Building. He raised his fist, my friend, but then let it down again. It occurred to me at that moment that we might actually escape this mess, provided the large youth was willing to let it pass. The spectators, all of them grinning bewhile, had thinned down to just three or four of the most evil of them. That was when a baldheaded policeman came forward suddenly out of nowhere and took the youth by his arm.

"This how you get your fun? Beating up little old men?"

"Little? I used to be six feet tall!"

By now there were just two persons watching the scene, treacherous people who convinced the constable that everything had been owing to me.

It fell out that we were conveyed, Earl and me, to the nearest police station and invited to sit among a throng of miscreants waiting to be processed. Even by contemporary standards, these were some of the worst people I had ever seen. By error I had been placed next to some sort of mixed-race woman weighing a good twenty stone or more and adorned with green lipstick. As if she might actually know how to use the thing, she held an early model proto-escrubilator in her lap. Two seats next to her I chanced to see three migrants, illegal probably, glancing about with darting eyes, prototypical Mexicans or Hondurans, or something of that kind. My mind fled back to the 1950s, before authentic Americans had been supplanted by . . . "Sewage," I call 'em. Arrest me if you can.

At length I did manage to find a place near the front, where no one else wished to be. Counting on my fingers up to eight and a half, I identified two whores whom no one in right mind could wish to penetrate, as also a representative number of cocaine/meth/heroin/serotonin/glue abusers. One man had allowed his snot to form a little river that ran over his bleeding lips and thence to the floor. Never would the world be any good again, not till the authorities were authorized to escrubilate *in situ* all such examples as these.

Where was Earl?

Calling upon my powers of concentration, and to escape these unpleasant precincts, I began mentally to conjugate a list of some twenty strong German verbs, avoiding only the future pluperfect. I scored poorly however, one more evidence of my deteriorating ability. From there I went on to articulate all the English kings starting with Alfred, the last of the good ones and by far the best. I strove to get through the periodic table, but my desiccated memory petered out with molybdenum. Finally, using appropriate finger movements, I tried to recall the seventeen primary knots that had won me my first merit badge.

It was after 11:20 that I was taken away to a narrow cell with two mismatched chairs in it. The interrogator was a heavy-set man, corpulent actually, with porcupine hair and a face suggestive of the most thoroughgoing brutality. I liked him at once. He gave me time to light up a cigarette before I said:

"There's hardly anything in this world I would less wish to do than be a source of concern to the police."

"That right?"

"Oh, yes! Civilization depends upon you people! People with an instinct for brutality. If I were in your place I'd be smashing heads *all day long.* Those little sticks you fellows carry, some of 'em have *lead* in 'em I understand. Like to have one myself."

The man relaxed. Not that he had not already been that way. I saw that he was close to smiling.

"You'd like to get in on that would you?" he asked. "Keeping the peace?"

"I can do without peace, if I could kill just one single stinking little . . ."

"Little bit old for that aren't you? You should of been with us back in '92. Bam! Smash! We had us a pretty good country back then, is what my old daddy used to say."

"I was there!"

We shook. He was willing to take a cigarette from me, a sanctioned action entailing important penalties.

"Who's that other fellow with you?"

"Earl?"

"How does he feel about all this stuff?"

"He hates it as much as I do!"

We managed to put Earl on his feet and prod him out into the open city. The district was full of apartment houses shaped like dominoes standing on end. Topple just the first one and the rest would all fall down. For one brief time I felt a surge of sympathy for all New Yorkers everywhere, whether in god-awful Canarsie or the hellish Bronx. And yet our policeman had somehow remained above it all, and proved himself a superior driver as he bore each of us to each other's home.

Twenty-Two

I had been doing well, fairly well, when I took a call

from K, indubitably the most pertinacious and hard-nosed personality of my acquaintance. The date was September first, and he was keen to have a meeting of The Four. We needed not merely to set an agenda for the forthcoming quarter, but also to amend our list of hate objects, subtracting some, adding others. Again he had begun to moot about eliminating certain categories, talk show hosts for example, pornographic actresses, basketball players, and other members of the American elite.

"Some of that trash has over a billion dollars!"

"I know."

"Well? Are we going to kill 'em, or not?"

"Simply a matter of priorities K."

"Well let me ask you this Howard—how many have we killed so far? And I'm not talking about cats neither!"

"Not many."

"'Not many,' he says. Be honest, Howard, for God's sake be honest."

We met on September second. There was no question but that Casper's apartment was the most threadbare, most undecorated, and most ill-situated domicile this side of East River. To ameliorate for that, Earl had brought his wife all the way from Queens.

We labored till late afternoon, which is to say until the woman had furnished us with blueberry muffins and a sectioned pink dish holding four kinds of marmalade, jelly, preserves, and some other condiment. She, too, was allowed to have some.

"I think we've done enough for one day," Casper offered. "We're just a bunch of old men after all, and we do get tired."

"*You* might be tired Casp, but don't try to speak for everybody."

We waited for the remark to fade and then finally to run away and join the huge storehouse of similar remarks that we had had to hear over the past twenty-seven months.

"Some of us are tired, some not. Alright? Can I see a show of hands?"

"What we need is some sort of vacation, don't you think? Get away from New York."

"I *like* New York."

We looked at him. It might even have been a sincere expression, though he wasn't willing to adhere to it for very long.

"Good time to visit the mountains."

"Or sea?"

"Why, yes."

We had a show of hands. Both those locations had therapeutic value, but the well-known annealing effect of sea water upon a person's hemorrhoids threw the vote that way.

"California?"

"Are you serious?"

"Florida?"

"I was thinking of the Mediterranean. But of course Casper could never afford anything like that."

"The blue Aegean!" said me, smacking my lips over certain classical scenes that had taken place in those blood-soaked waters.

"You? You have trouble enough negotiating your bath-tub."

"Florida then. Hell, we could drive that far."

Twenty-Three

Autumn in Brooklyn, but raining in Queens. It was to my advantage that I owned two suitcases, one of them for medicine and the other for cultural equipment. The sound of footsteps in the hall, or finding that someone had been tampering with my mail and I could have fled my apartment carrying just less than 48.3 pounds in books, discs, pharmaceuticals, and stock certificates.

It was the third suitcase, the grand one, that was needed for Florida. It hadn't been used in years, and still smelt of the Amalfi Coast when finally I forced it open. I spied a dried-up cigarette trying to get out of view, but instead of destroying the thing as the laws required, I ignited and sucked on it for as long as I dared. The walls had ears, the roaches had eyes, and the television set had an uncanny way of pivoting in my direction no matter how adroitly I sought to evade its rays. Entranced by the lovely woman giving the news, I was put in mind of those little creatures, your protozoan *hydras* who expel waste material through their mouths.

I made sure to pack my swimming trunks, my fishing equipment, my wet suit and snorkeling apparatus. I chose just sixteen books to bring along, a painful decision that left me with a thirteenth-century bestiary and that demonology acquired all those weeks ago in narrow Vermont. Of music, I brought Kaufman's *Parsifal,* one of Palestrina, and three Patti Page songs recorded when she and the nation were at their best. Also Mahler's *Eighth* of course, save that I had taken care to erase the first movement. All great artists are allowed to make mistakes.

I packed my life insurance policies, one of them in favor of ------------- and the other designating an Alabama Boxer Dog Rescue Service. Spare glasses I brought, as also a fair amount of some very colorful beachwear showing mermaids and dolphins and the sort. By habit I started to bring some of my erectile dysfunction capsules as well, before recollecting that these were themselves dysfunctional in my current state. In any event I had already put together more than another forty-five pounds of stuff and by no means would Casper—it was his car—have allowed me more.

The gizmo? I wrapped it in Christmas paper, a comical

action analogous to giving poisoned candy to a child, or a length of rope to office workers in New York. I was quite cheerful, though I knew I'd get no sleep that night. Suddenly I jumped out of bed, dismayed that I could have forgot to provide for my chameleons and the creature (a mouse?) that lived beneath the bed.

Contrary to expectations, I did sleep (briefly) and then came awake to the noise of unspeakable music issuing from an Hispanic automobile passing in the street. I could read, or take a pill, or pretend that I was sleeping; in the actual event I was startled just then by a call from K, who wanted me to talk him off to sleep.

"Hmm," he said. "Wonder what Casp is doing."

"Getting his car ready I suppose. Fuel and oil."

"Oh, no, please don't tell me we're using that old beat-up heirloom of his!"

"I just hope it'll carry four people."

"Four minus one leg."

"Actually he does rather well. For the kind of person he is. Well I'll say goodbye now. Need to get some sleep."

"I want a window seat, OK? And I'm bringing an empty bottle to piss in."

"Bring four. Well, see you in the morning. Big day ahead."

"I know you're trying to get rid of me. I can tell."

"And besides, they're *all* window seats. Think about it."

"Maybe you should leave the gizmo behind."

"What! You been to Florida recently? They got more targets than Wall Street!"

Finally I fell asleep, if you wish to call it that, but only to be disturbed a second time by a call from the most nervous man in the group.

"Howard?"

"Yes?"

"It's only a vacation, right? This is most definitely *not* the time to start killing people, and I'm sure you agree with that."

"Bring money. Casper doesn't have any."

"You know, in some ways we're on vacation all the time. None of us work."

"Ah? And so the gizmo produced itself?"

"Might be better if it hadn't."

"It didn't!"

"Oh, right."

Etc.

I knew that by a certain time I'd be waiting at the curb for an archaic car with an archaic man in it. Supposedly I was the leader of this association, and yet K was already on board and sitting next to the driver. It was a good mechanic certainly, the one who had modified this car for one-legged drivers. Operated by voice commands, the vehicle incorporated both the newest and the oldest technology anywhere to be seen brought together "synergistically," as in were, each with each. The floor had holes in it, but the disc player was the most advanced in the world.

We drove slowly down Ewell Street, perhaps the most notorious route in the city. Came next 62nd Avenue, a much better road bordered with high price shops so discrete and unadorned that I, certainly, couldn't imagine what was going on in those places. It was a minimalistic period in America's irrefragable on-going development of a better and better world offering pricier and pricier clothes. Almost laughed out loud when I espied a female manikin disporting herself in a space age ensemble made, seemingly, of aluminum. The next I knew we had penetrated into Earl's neighborhood, his very street indeed, and then Earl himself with a large red velvet carpetbag standing at his side. He was smiling. The day really was fresh and bright and only very slightly a bit too hot. Next to Earl stood Earl's wife.

"Oh, boy. Wasn't it you Howie, who said we'd each

have his own window seat?"

I admitted that it was. "She can sit in my lap. Wouldn't bother me at all."

"No! I don't imagine it would. But what about *my* lap?"

"She shall sit," said I definitively, "in Earl's lap."

They grumbled. I could see insubordination aborning in their faces. In the end she sat exactly between her husband and me, where the two of us could revel in her perfume, her gaiety, and general persona withal. A long time since my withered old knee had been in actual touch with that of a fifty-year-old female still in season. I were fond of old Earl, but would happily have used the gizmo on him to transform *his* wife into mine.

We had not traveled four blocks before we were halted by a security car parked sideways across the road. We didn't blame the agents. They were required to stop a certain number of old white males, or else lose their jobs for focusing too much on guilty people. Putting on pleasant faces, we exited the car and began emptying our pockets, our suitcases, our carpetbag, our purse and glove compartment. Affirmative action beneficiaries, they took apart Gwen's tube of lipstick but ignored the gizmo.

"Where you goin'?" the tallest and most terrifying of them asked.

"Florida."

"Say what?"

"So we can join up with lots of other old people like us."

"OK, that's alright I guess. You folks play shuffleboard?" He had dropped the lipstick into the evidence bag. Meantime his partner was photographing us from various angles. The carpetbag, as it happened, held all manner of pharmaceuticals and the agent was bound in duty to take specimens of each kind. That was when K made the egregious error of offering a bribe.

"We have all this liquor," he said. "More than we can

use. Why don't you take one of these bottles for yourselves? You deserve it after all your hard work."

"Say what?"

"Hard work."

"Whoa. How 'bout I break that firkin bottle over yo'
fuckin' head and stick it up yo' lilly-white mother-fuckin'
ass white boy? How you like that—ten to twenty in the
goddamn mother-fuckin' Feral pen?"

"No, no; that's not what I was suggesting. Mother-
fucking pen? Count me out. Whew!"

"Motha-fuckin' spooks. You come in here and do like
that? Shiiit!"

"We have money."

"I ain't talkin' no money! I'm talkin' Feral pen! You feel
me? How much you got man?"

"I could let you have . . . Twenty?"

"Shiiit! Twenty shiiit. Shit, I don' need yo' mother-
fuckin' money!"

The other man now spoke up:

"It's a *contribution* Leroy! Know what I'm sayin'? Shiiit
man, take it."

We paid. Another dozen cars were now lined up behind us and were honking their mother-fucking horns at
us.

In order to move southward, we had at first to aim
northward. We had agreed to keep a tight watch on the
driver, who had lately begun showing signs of Alzheimer
syndrome. New York of course comprised any number of
townships, each with a little name of its own. God forgive
me, I was never able to specify the moment I left one and
entered another. Paradise Garden appeared just in front of
us, a ramshackle place that would have been more comfortable in Tanzania. We sped past it as fast as we could,
ignoring the insults directed either at us or perhaps the
car. That was when K made another of his uncalled-for
remarks.

"It's just as well Casper, that you have all those diseases instead of one of us. After all, you've only got one leg and your eye is no good, and so you're used to it. Suffering, I mean."

The woman bent forward and smote the bastard on the head. "You're the worst person I've ever known," she said.

"Maybe so, maybe so. A good physicist however."

Ahead we suddenly descried another roadblock up ahead, a huge nuisance for people wishing to flee the city, the county, even the state. We feared at first our driver might try to smash through it; instead, he turned sharply right and carried out a brilliant procedure that no one with an average mind would have dared. The whole group broke out into applause.

"I take it back," K allowed. "You're a goddamn genius Casp!" he said, pouring and passing a goblet of dark red wine to the man.

"We all are. Geniuses."

"Not me," the woman said.

"Thank heavens for that. One more would be too many by much."

We were now in a trajectory that would carry us to Maine. The coastal city of Seamore appeared on the right-hand side, an archetypical hostel for people attached economically to New York City. It inspired us to turn about and aim for Florida once again. The ride was hindered by potholes, and we ended up, most of us, with wine on our clothes. In any case it was nearly noon by now, time for our sandwiches. Casper hadn't brought any.

The music, too, was exceptional. K had brought along a recording of Glenn Campbell's *Southern Nights* as also two variant versions of Shchedrin's *Trombone Concerto*, one of them massively better than the other. Next was Strauss' *Heldenleben*, played for my benefit. Casper preferred Mozart. We could and should have left him where we were, had only he not been driving. That was when we came

into an Australasian district, a primitive locality full of
some of history's most uninvestigated hominids.

This time the roadblock was staffed by an assortment
of people—two Haitians, a large woman in boots and sun-
glasses, and a mature man who looked so much like one
of my favorite old-time cartoon characters that I couldn't
help chortling out loud. He didn't like that.

"You got a problem?" he respectfully inquired.

"No, no, not at all."

He came nearer. By God, he really did resemble that
person, a heavy-set individual who used to go about
mounted on a dinosaur. He came still nearer.

"Now you aren't going to throw *that* up at me are you?"

"No, no. I don't actually read newspapers anymore,
much less the comic section."

"Wine?" Earl offered, pouring a generous helping for
the man. Suddenly he drew his wife's skirt down to cover
her knees.

"Anyway, where do you think you're going in this old
heap? What is this, a Hudson for God's sakes?"

"A Kaiser!" Casp retorted. "Or Frasier maybe."

The man laughed, a good sign. The woman in the sun
glasses had lost interest in us, and the other two had put
away their pistols. Already our fuel was low, and we'd not
likely get entirely out of the city without investing in some
very expensive xylol.

We drove slowly up one side and down the other of
that enchanted isle, stopping at intersections policed either by some of the new generation of robots or their human imitations. We halted for an elderly woman who
thought she recognized our car. We stared at each other.
This was an old-style woman, I divined, who had seen
what post-modernity looks like and had declined to par-
ticipate. I wanted to kiss her. We passed slowly by the site
where the buildings that replaced The Twin Towers were
being replaced. A fat man on a motorcycle just then came

up abreast and, smiling evilly, grabbed for Casper's cigarette. Had only we had air conditioning in that old car, we could have gone to Florida with our windows closed. Cigarette? K suddenly yanked the thing from Casper's mouth and disposed of it before any of the pedestrians had reported us. Three minutes later we had parked at the very tip of Manhattan and were waiting for the ferry.

It was a capacious vessel, mostly flat, and the ferryman had a confidence-inspiring face. By this time we were immune to the laughter and gasps incited by the sight of our unusual car. Moving carefully, Casper boarded the ferry and parked between a high-price Jaguar and a Kazakhstani product with a coon tail furling from the antenna. These days the Statue of Liberty no longer held a torch aloft but rather some other symbol inspired by the Walt Disney organization.

"What is *that*!" asked Earl.

"God wot."

"God wot not!"

"God wot not what."

The bay was choppy, but even so we managed to arrive in good time at Staten Island, a deforested place crowded with skin jobs, wetbacks, homunculi, somnambulists, and at least one giant golem seven feet high. These were the constituents of the place, along with abnormal structures shaped like those old-time cigarette packages standing upright when they should have been lying on one side.

"And yet," I said, "Saint Anthony lived in a shack made of two or three rocks standing on top of each other, enough to keep the scorpions at bay. I think everyone should live in a shack."

"I do live in a shack!"

Just then on one of the upper stories I spied a young girl framed in a pane of glass. Why so sad? She was only a thousand miles or so from brooks with trout in them, not to mention trees and green pastures. Worn down by unabridged ugliness in every direction, we were tired, we four, and must have looked like we had been victimized about ten seconds ago by a gizmo attack. It didn't help to see a teenage whore made up to look like Cleopatra, an epiphenomenon that no doubt seemed normal to those weaned on them.

We drove up onto the shores of New Jersey and after submitting to X-rays and an ineffective metal detector that noticed my cigarette lighter but not my Beretta, sped off at about fifteen miles the hour toward Apalachicola.

Twenty-Four

We had prepared for everything. We were not however prepared to find long columns of recent immigrants migrating southward with their belongings. Pathetic scene, women pushing baby carriages, overheated dogs, wounded men in unclean bandages. On the bright side, we knew that this was nothing that a more tolerant and more broadminded, a more compassionate and versatile social welfare policy couldn't solve. Me, I wanted to slaughter the lot of 'em.

By noon we had broken into the state of Pennsylvania, a rectangular province with barns here and cities there, and withal the same sort of blinkered humanity, judging from them, that had overspread all the northern colonies.

"Look at that one," said K, nodding toward an especially nonplussing post-modern man or perhaps woman. "See? His face has that stamped quality of vicious . . . That vicious quality . . . Look at him."

"You want to wake up Earl?"

The man indeed was sleeping, his poor old head at peace in the lap of his therapeutic wife. Typical of him, this pampered man, to have passed out in the midst of the supernal music now playing on the machine.

"He needs to pee," the woman said.

"He's sleeping!"

"That doesn't mean he doesn't need to pee."

"How can you tell?"

"Never mind about that. Can we stop?"

"Here," said I, reaching an empty bottle to her. (And what, pray, were we to use when it came *her* time to pass fluid? K's baseball cap?)

"No, I'd have to wake him up. Can't we stop?"

"Good God woman, he'll have to wake up in any case!"

"You don't know him like I do. He's shy, and can't pee in his own presence."

Nevertheless we drove on for another few miles before veering off onto the shoulder of the highway, a propitious place owing to the roadside billboards offering privacy. Three of us—it needed three—three of us walked Earl the forty yards to the nearest sign where we astonished a middle-age woman doing her own business in the shade. She shrieked.

We passed to the next sign where, however, a long black snake got up suddenly on its haunches and sizzled at us. The third effort brought us to a billboard promoting a brand of hair oil, where we came to a stop. There was a considerable rubbish in the shade, including what looked to me like a miniature fetus in a mason jar. Here Earl pissed, still snoring while his wife shook him off and tucked him back into place.

These were desperate times, these dying summer days, and the sun itself seem to bode great bale for the remains of our two-thousand-year-old civilization. Up until now the roadside advertisements had been more or less per-functory, not greatly unlike what was seen in the 1950s. Up until now. Really, had it come to this, that every hu-man activity must be organized for money and/or sex? That every youth should wear on his face the proof of his own soul's decease, had it inevitably come to this? That human quality and prolonged prosperity never may coexist? Had I been speaking out loud?

"This is supposed to be a *vacation* Howie. If you can't be cheerful, maybe you ought not be at all."

"Well just think how *I* feel," K said, "having to be the leader of all you gloomy people. I never wanted the job in the first place."

We went forward. Casper was getting tired, and his driving had deteriorated woefully over the past hour. He attempted to avoid a large green turtle, but ended up slaying the thing in the right-hand lane. At this distance from New York, the stream of refugees was not one-fifth as dense as just an hour ago, a deficiency that atoned for itself in terms of the roadside litter. We dodged pieces of household furniture, a refrigerator, and other equipment discarded in the roadway itself. A late-model car had run off the road and had continued deep into a sorghum field where it lay upside down with fumes emanating from at least two places. We were still within a radius of Philadelphia, and the influences of that city lay all about. We passed a shopping mall, a massive development equipped with a Ferris wheel and a giant stature of Johnny Appleseed made of plastic. The American Democracy, composed largely of fat women in tight pants and adolescents wearing baseball caps, democracy was flourishing everywhere a person chose to look.

Wanting coffee, we turned into a franchised restaurant holding more than the average number of slobs with their shirttails hanging out. The place offered twenty-four grinds of coffee, including two from Thailand. The clientele may have been proletarians, most of them, but what a number of connoisseurs were in that place! I counted six negroes, four Mestizos, and a deranged man drawing pictures in the air.

That was when K strode to my side, his calico face full of worry.

"Ahhh, hate to tell you this Howard, but it looks like someone has taken the gizmo."

"You say that to me?"

"Next time maybe you won't wrap it up like a Christmas present."

I knew that I had fainted when I saw people bending over me, one of them fanning me with a magazine.

We went in five different directions. The gizmo was relatively too large for the thief to hide in his pocket and the crowd too exiguous for the malefactor to lose himself among others of his type. Gwen went direct to the nearest women's shop and checked each and every dressing room, while her husband went from place to place, irritating people with threats and accusations. Casper of course wasn't capable of a great deal, but earned our respect by putting to use his one good eye. Meantime K had disappeared, and I was having trouble with my revolver. The thing was supposed to hold six shells, but somehow in the process of travel two of them had lost themselves. There was about as much chance of recovering them as of a whole raft of other impossible things.

Somewhere in this confusion of stores and streets, the most powerful man in the world was scampering off with the most portentous piece of loot since Helen's time. Minutes were passing. I hastened back to the Frasier, checked beneath it, replaced the lost cartridges, and then opened the brandy and gulped at it greedily.

We must have wasted a full forty-five minutes in these pursuits when K, to curtail a long and highly detailed story, appeared around the corner (a goofy-looking smile on his already goofy face), while transporting in the crook of his arm a brightly-colored and well-wrapped Christmas present. We cheered for him, urging him forward across the last short distance that divided him from the car and us.

"He did it!" (I can't recall who said that.) "Son-of-a-bitch, he's the best man here!" (Not my comment.) "Give the man a drink!"

Still smiling, K gave the inestimable thing over into my keeping. But then drew it back again when he recollected who was mostly at fault for having lost it in the first place.

"Let Gwen have it. That great big purse of hers."

The purse indeed was great and held artifacts that hadn't been seen in years. I stood by silently as she tried but failed to find room in her bag among the pencils and passports and .22 automatic. Larger than the Antikythera Mechanism, we finally had to hide the gizmo in the largest of her several trunks.

"Entirely appropriate," said Casper, "that the fate of the world be at the caprice of a girl."

It was now 2:17 (p.m.), too late in the day to listen to K detail the whole story of how he had saved the gizmo. Even so, he kept elongating the narration, hoping to conserve as far as possible his current prestige. Thinking back over his achievement, he began smacking his lips in a way that was particularly unpleasant.

"Quite simple," he said, "what I did. Surprises me that none of you were able to think of it."

"What did you do?"

"All you geniuses. I realize we're on vacation, but even so."

"What did you do?"

"Hmm?"

"How did you find the gizmo!"

He shrugged. "Deduction, that's all. And persistence. Maybe a little bit of educated instinct, too. Try it sometime."

There were three of us, four including the girl, and although he was still somewhat formidable in his old age, I have no doubt we could have done things to him, even without resorting to the gizmo.

We moved on. The quality of Earl's driving had so eroded that his woman had taken on the job herself. She was prudent and skillful and obeyed all the laws, but her average speed made me want to scream. I used the time to catch up with my log, filling two full pages with the events of that day.

Twenty-Five

By nightfall we had reached a specific location identified both on the map and in reality as a town called *Mo-har-rou* after the original inhabitants. The site of two famous skirmishes, it was thought that at least sixty-eight aborigines and as many as three colonialists had met their destinies in this place. We passed a roadside attraction where a fat woman was vending adult material and busts of the supposed Tutankhamen in various sizes. But we never stopped for any of this. Earl had brought out his picnic basket, and we were peacefully passing back and forth the biscuits and pickles and choice pieces of fried chicken. Apart from the liver, the chicken comprised white meat only. Conscious of calories, we had discarded the skins while taking advantage of the mustard and mayonnaise, a vinegary slaw, a sliced tomato, and as many chocolate chip cookies as a person could want until the supply ran out. I have sampled dishes fetched by snotty waiters in high price restaurants, yes and I have gulped down raw oysters harvested by hand from shallow bays. I have been to France and come back again. I have tasted quail endued with nutmeg, also salads composed of snails, avocado, and artichoke hearts. All these I have sampled at various moments in my traveled life, but not one such meal was in any way superior to a certain Italian dish described in Latin by a mostly forgotten eighteenth-century author in Earl's library collection.

The night was dark and the music Shostakovich's. Very few refugees could still be seen, and even these were committed to keeping out of the light beams of Casper's car. Not without sympathy I caught view of a Caucasian female lying face up in a field of weeds. (As if her thin blanket could ward away the dew!) Still, it is worth remembering that at one time her nationality had enjoyed equal standing in many of the states.)

Earl was sleeping, his wife was driving, and the rest of us, save for myself alone, were getting drowsy. I say "myself" and "alone" because I had become fascinated with a long series of radio towers that seemed to mark the edge of the world in that direction. Especially I homed in on a far-away cerulean-blue and somewhat granular light that seemed to me, with my uncommon sensibility, to be frantically relaying vital information out to the countryside and ships at sea. Really, could anything be more plangent than that? Messages from the land of death running at light speed over the wrinkled topography? Rumors of foreign invasion? Oncoming traffic bringing the latest information? And always that abnormal bat running side by side with us, mile after mile. And then, to add wonder to magic, the sight of a hanged man silhouetted against the moon. I could not know what thoughts the others were having, except that they were always much less imaginative than mine.

Looking back on it from the safety of later times, I began to regret that I had wasted such a portion of my life during daylight hours. Night was the thing. Velvety night that cloaks reality—all good things happen in the dark— and supplies the perfect medium for gazing deeply into, for example, a woman's eyes. Blue lights! Far away lights at the end of the world, an important reason for remaining alive. Of course that was when K, the essential philistine, spoke up loud and clear:

"About time to find a motel I suppose."

"No," I said. "No, I think we can go on for another little bit."

"Oh, hell. Is he watching those lights again?"

"Hey! There's a place just ahead."

"No. No, I don't think that's for us. Not really."

She left the highway, Earl's woman, and parked expertly between two motorcycles with people on them. The motel, if that's what it was, was of a well-known franchise that bore the logo of a full-figured women in profile. And then, too, there was a restaurant associated with the place, and we could see a scattering of some all-too-ordinary-looking people bending over their feed.

"Let's keep driving," I recommended.

The receptionist was a decent-looking type who might well have served as the model for the company's logo. But we had not prepared ourselves for the interview that awaited us. We were willing to complete the necessary forms, but were taken aback by some of the questions:

"Are you still at -------------?" (She mentioned my exact address.)

"Why yes. How did you know?"

"No recurrence of shingles?"

"No, no."

"Gastric problems?"

"No, no, no. That was a long time ago."

"Are you transporting any livestock, pets, or seed plants?"

"I do have a couple of Jackson Chameleons. But my neighbor is looking after them."

"'Couple'?"

"OK, four."

"Do you have any firearms on your persons? Or in your vehicle?"

"Certainly not!" I lied.

"Childhood psychoses?"

At this question we had to draw off a few feet in order to consult about it. Finally:

"A few. But most of them were simply neuroses."

"Are you now or have you ever been a member of a White Nationalist party as defined in the Uniformity Act of 2017?"

"He is!" said K, pointing at me. In fact his own memberships were at least as problematic as mine.

"Are you vaccinated . . . ?"

"Yes."

". . . against the new diseases?" (She offered us a list of those diseases, most of them dealing with attitudinal problems.)

"And have you volunteered to bequeath your organs for transplantation procedures? And if not, why not?"

"At our ages? Who would want 'em?"

"Now please list your college training, if any, and the number of absentee days."

She was not unkindly however, and after chiding us briefly for a number of things, she unlocked the door and permitted us into a long narrow hall hung with obscene photographs. Themselves, the rooms were more than adequate and in addition to the bidets were provided with mirrored ceilings and a heart-shaped bed with pink satin sheets. Even so, Gwen insisted on a separate room for her partner and herself. We bade them goodnight, but then had immediately to go back and hold Earl on his feet while he urinated. Let me admit right away that I was not overly delighted about sharing a room with two superannuated geniuses of uncertain hygienic habits. Right away Casper hobbled to the TV, much chagrined to find that it demanded fifteen dollars per hour for ordinary viewing plus twenty-five more for looking into the other rooms. On the other hand the roses were free, and the jar of lubricants had hardly been used.

It wasn't so awful. K had fallen off to sleep right away and was muttering to himself in a polite sort of way. Now and again I might catch a word or two, but made no further effort to understand him once I realized he was speaking in a South Slavic tongue. As for Casper, he had gone to bed bareheaded while dressed in an odd-looking apparel representing itself as a set of pajamas. His tie was blue, and from his book there protruded a chit of toilet paper employed as a bookmark.

"What are you reading?" I respectfully inquired.

He turned and looked at me. "Do I ask what *you're* reading?"

"No."

"Then let that be the end of it."

(Truth was, I could see the text, or anyway the chapter headings, in the overhead mirror.)

"Damn, Casp! Are you still captivated by that writer? He's as obsolete as your other favorite philosopher."

He turned and looked at me. There was a good deal of traffic out on the highway, including intermittent trucks built by the Dacia corporation, judging from them. I did not have to go to the window to get a view of the drivers. I knew spontaneously what sort they were.

"Really, what do they want Casp, all these working people? More beer? Ten-hour football games on large screen television?"

"Would you just kindly shut up? It's hard enough just trying to get everyone in bed. Don't know why I ever agreed to it, being the leader of this group."

I returned to my own book, a delicious edition of one of the more neglected historians of the Kwarezmian regime. It was difficult stuff, I admit it, plodding through that syncretic tongue. Bloody days, those, when rulers would amputate a person's legs for the least infractions. Archeologists had spent four seasons at the main site before having finally to admit that the culture hadn't been worth even the initial enquiry. Find a copy of the report of that dig and you can retire at a very young age. Three copies known to exist.

I woke two hours later with my eyes still bearing on my

book. It was my method—to summon up a medley of
dreams and readings and allow myself to soak for various
durations in the brew. Was this a feat my colleagues could
have achieved? Not in a pig's ass it was.

Twenty-Six

We awoke all at the same moment and then, in spite of
the tumult in the hall, went back to sleep again. But even
in dreams I could hear the signatures of the modern
world—trucks with imperfect brakes, chain saws, television sets, and screams coming from the rooms. Where
now, I ask, were the roosters of yesterday, the flowing
brooks, the love songs of whippoorwills? Yes, and someday the present world will undergo such changes as to
bring the whole modern world to an end.

Next came breakfast, a rescue operation involving fried
eggs and for the first time in years, actual grits. There were
all sorts of juices on the table, including a pitcher of a dark
fluid I couldn't immediately, or even later, convincingly
identify. It did prove helpful in washing down the fifteen
or twenty pharmaceuticals collectively in use. Casper, to
start with him, needed all sorts of odd-shaped pills and
capsules that he tried, very foolishly, to swallow all at the
same time.

"What is that one for?" I asked, indicating a diamond-
shaped medication with a trademark on it.

"You sure you want to discuss this? During breakfast?"

I hushed. I had my own medicines, and yes my own illnesses too, and no, I didn't care to discuss them either. Or
not until K emptied out a capsule as big almost as his
thumb and began licking at it.

"Gad!" I said. (Others of us said "Good Lord!" or made
similar exclamations.)

"What on earth is *that* for?"

"Hair growth," he said unhesitatingly.

"You got more hair than you need!"

The man was unashamed. With one swift move he lifted his wig and allowed us one by one to come near and touch his indeed glabrous pate. It shone, that cranium, like chromium, save that this one contained, or anyway used to contain, some of the best intellectual resources this side of the River James.

Back on the road again! But instead of stars and planets, the goddamn sun was exuding a peculiarly bilious sort of light that got into a person's eyes and gave him a headache. Worse, it allowed us to see things that in a more intolerant and more decent world would have been against the law—fat women in tight pants, shopping malls, suntan salons, negroes with bones in their noses, pornography boutiques, fifteen-year-old girls striving (and succeeding!) to look like whores, indeed the whole landscape of classical America. I reached for the gizmo and succeeded finally in tearing it from Casper's grasp. Really, weren't it an act of mercy to put an end to a society as ill as this?

"Really," I asked aloud, "wouldn't it be an act of mercy to put an end to a society as ill as this?"

"It's their world Howard, not ours. You must accept the popular culture, if you want to be happy."

"I'd more lief be dead."

"Yes, that sounds like you. You're an egotist Howie, a stark egotist."

"Possibly. Actually I'd rather kill the whole lot of 'em. And start over again."

"Why yes, maybe we could pick up with Elizabethan London and proceed anew."

"Me, I'd much rather . . . Holy Toledo, look at that one!"

We slowed and looked. It was a middle age man with a braided pigtail, gaudy earrings, and a rhinestone purse with a hair dryer sticking out.

"Glad my parents didn't live to see this."

"College professor. Want to bet?"

"Let's do some things to him, want to? There's four of us."

"Five actually."

"No seriously, this might be our best chance."

Instead we were taken around the block by Gwen and brought to a parking space in front of a shop that specialized in antiquarian beer cans and comic books. I admit that I entered the place and glanced around at the rubbish, coming away a few moments later with an inexpensive watercolor signed by a certain "Philip," a good-intentioned artist devoid of excessive skill. Vacations are useless without at least one superfluous purchase. The canvas was a full twenty-four inches square, an impediment that couldn't easily find space for itself inside the already-crowded car. Earl, deteriorating by the minute, had actually invested in one of the beer cans, a famous brand still sometimes found on the outskirts of football stadiums and your old-time outdoor movie theaters. We had to escort him to the car and wait around uselessly till he had gifted the can to his embarrassed wife.

Half an hour later we came suddenly upon a stretch of the highway where north-bound migrants were more often to be seen than those moving south. Was it possible? That the country had begun to sort itself out in accord with natural inclinations? That the South might once again be a normal place while the north more and more enriched itself with feminists and queers and members of secondary races?

Meantime the right rear tire had lost its pressure, the third time since dawn. Gwen would need the better part of an hour to blow it up again, and by now our beer supply was down to the last few bottles. We could read, we could argue, we could do neither; in the actual event, two of us quickly fell off to sleep again.

Concerning myself alone, I woke just as we were passing through a certain *Perth Amboy*, a historic site named, as I later came to understand, after two brothers bearing unusual names. The place itself was entirely generic for a town in that location, and I was much relieved that our tires hadn't again given out on us at that moment. We hurried through the eastern district, a dilapidated quarter full of racial elements, and then after following our chosen highway all the way to the end, we turned to the left, and to the sea.

And so this then was what the driver had in store for us—to grant us a vacation not so much in Florida as in a small New Jersey village known as *Sea Bright*. We protested of course, but the woman could not be made to change her mind.

"Sea Bright? Hell, we might as well have stayed in Amboy!"

"Or even Perth."

"Want me to take you back?"

"My God woman! Why are you treating us this way?"

"I paid dear," said Casper, our most impecunious member, "for a brand-new swimming suit. Yea, and fishing equipment, too!"

She turned calmly and looked at each of us in turn. "Florida? This old car won't go that far."

"Old, she says? 'Old'? This is a *good* car goddamn it! And it's not even as old as me!"

The village, as noted, really was quite small, and the water that lapped the asphalt had an opaque quality. We moved slowly past Harry's Lobster House and at the following intersection turned down to the shore where right away Earl descried a loaded diaper drifting back and forth. It were I who first remarked on a small white crab dragging a hypodermic needle to a hole in the sand.

"What did you expect?" someone said. "After all Howie, we're still in spitting distance of your favorite town."

"Yep, this is where it empties out, the sewage system that starts in Times Square."

It wasn't Florida, it wasn't even California, but there was a lot of ocean out there, and we were free to behold it. Which is to say until a certain dangerous-looking element in a male's bikini hove up in front of us, asking:

"Where yo' badges? You gots to have badges bitch. Where is they?"

"We don't need no stinking badges!" uttered K, before suddenly regretting the outburst and putting on an apologetic face. "Where can we get them?" he continued sweetly.

"Git 'em at the gitting place! Sheet mon, not my job to follow you around. You feel me?"

The getting place turned out to be a federal office just next to Giglio's Bait and Tackle. Inside we found two female attendants, a Japanese and a Chinese, who plainly disliked each other. Yes, and someday the whole country will dislike each other. We paused to read a bulletin affixed to the wall in which the prohibitions against discrimination, homophobia, possession of fireworks, and tobacco use were spelled out to the last codicil. Clothing was required, save in cases of religious belief.

"We'd like to buy those badges," said Earl, "if we need them."

"If you need them?" (She was Vietnamese, not Chinese. We apologized.)

"How you think you no need them? Special deal, yes? White people? I think so, yes."

We apologized. The Japanese woman had turned away and was looking out over the wrong ocean to her island home. She was so small, her precious little feet dangled an inch or two above the floor. As for the badges, dish-size artifacts bearing the image of the American eagle with blood-stained talons, they cost the exaggerated sum of $225 for the five of us. Plus an additional surcharge in favor of crippled veterans of the oil wars.

"How long are these good for?" one of us, K I believe it was, respectfully inquired.

"What you say! OK wise fellow, I see what you say. OK, I write!" And indeed she did take out an account book of some sort and begin to inscribe some of her national runes in it.

"No, no, I was just asking! For example, how long are these badges valid, as it were?"

"Oh." (She checked her watch, a clanging instrument not greatly larger than a dime.) "Six 'clock."

"Six o'clock!"

"What I say. You hear no good?"

"But . . . but how if we want to stay longer?"

"No!" (She had shaped her right hand into a really quite good simulacrum of a western style revolver.) "Bang!"

In the event, we produced another $125, some of which went into her purse. These funds should have given us roughly 28 hours for exploring the sand and water and the litter cast away all those years ago by the revelers of Jones Beach.

We feasted that night at The Crab Bucket, a dark place serviced by a family of Portuguese and/or Brazilians who really did share a somewhat crustacean-like facial cast. Beer was available, but the crabs were aged and gave off a disturbing smell. Under the circumstances we asked for vegetarian platters, but even here there were problems that caused Gwen to rise and go back to her room.

Rooms: We had paid in advance for a suite that offered mirrors not just on the ceiling but all four walls as well. Unfortunately the place had not been cleaned, and the tub was full of water holding a day's catch of still-living eels, or something of that genus. Apparently the tenants had departed in a hurry, leaving the eels behind in lieu of pay. Earl and me, we spent a god-awful time capturing the creatures in our hands and then transporting them one by one down to the sea. Asked to grade our vacation so far, we placed it at about a "one" on the group's ten-scale.

Supper at The Crab Bucket: The vegetables had included a recipe of ecologically prepared seaweed in aspic, the effective cause of Gwen's departure. We weren't easily able to characterize the clientele of that restaurant, save that it comprised some score of Asians, Africans, and Latin Americans, the overflow (said Casper wittily) of Raspail's great novel. I might not have the gizmo with me; I did however have my revolver. I looked for and found it precisely where it was supposed to be.

Twenty-Seven

If one especially wants to feel sympathy for us four old men, he is encouraged herewith to do so. Our money was running out, and Earl had lost his badge between two cracks in the boardwalk. Adding to our difficulties, the salt sea water was having deleterious effects on K's psoriasis and Earl's testosterone patch. Someone's wig was drifting out to sea. Casper, fearing sharks, had brought the gizmo into the water with him. Worse yet, seawater was leaching into Casper's hollow wooden leg, endangering the only typed copy of our redacted constitution. I don't mention my own problems.

First, my eyes were no good, my liver was worse, and I suffered from tinnitus, COPD, and vitreous flaking. The waves and ripples, they came and went, and the earth moved beneath my feet. One had constantly to lift one's foot, lest the whole leg sink up to one's knees in the sand. I saw a fleet of barges from New York City, but couldn't begin to count the number of crushed automobiles being offloaded into the sea. That was when the hindquarters of a hoofed animal of some rather considerable size bobbed to the surface where K was swimming. Worse, I suppose, was Casper's quandary when his crutch broke off in the turmoil of two closely following waves.

Even old men dislike being humiliated in front of comely girls in two-piece bathing suits. Or even one piece indeed. Our part was to obey Earl's intelligent wife, who by unanimous consent had been drafted to the leadership role. With tourists all about, I daren't emerge from the water and allow my revolver to be seen. Old men! We had spent so many years being young, it was dispiriting to have that privilege taken away and given over to others so much less experienced at that than us. This is where the sympathy comes in.

And then on Thursday arrived the jellyfish.

We wasted $300 on a man who claimed to be a car mechanic, another $450 on a "doctor" educated in Jamaica, and then $200 each on a fishing guide whose boat, it developed, was devoid of toilet facilities. Finally on Monday, with our wallets pretty well exhausted, we sat side by side on the beach and graded the vacationers passing by.

"Imagine you'd never seen one of these things" (humans) "before," said K. "Think how appalling the sight would be."

We turned and looked at Casper, the most unattractive of all us four.

"Look at that one," said Morgan. (Morgan? Another old man who had joined us at some point. A suspicious looking man, we were never during our whole association with him to discover what he was so suspicious of.) "She doesn't realize how good she looks in that bathing suit."

"Oh, she knows alright. And she does it on purpose, too!"

"Can't be. That's would be *vanity* you're talking about."

"They swim so much better with their buttocks hanging out, is that the way it works nowadays?"

"Cheez, look at *that* guy!"

This referred to a middle-aged fellow, hugely over-weight, who just didn't care anymore. We liked him at once.

"He knows what life is."

"Oh? And what is that, K?"

"Atoms. I thought you knew. A maelstrom of atoms taking on human shape."

"Right. Now for example you take this fat fellow with his bright red nipples . . ."

The fat fellow turned and looked at us.

"He's been around. He knows that no matter how hard a person tries, he knows what it comes down to in the end."

"Yes, and that daughter he so much adored, what's she up to now? A masseuse in San Francisco?"

"What daughter?" Morgan asked. (A less intelligent man than the rest of us, he couldn't envision anyone who wasn't standing just in front of him at the time. Pornography is wasted on such people, as also speech, eye charts, and travel brochures.)

"Very probably. And married to a business major."

"Oh, I get it," Morgan added. "Y'all are just making it up and talking about it."

I was sensible of flies crawling between my toes. I swear I could not remember problems of this sort when I was twenty-one. The sun, smaller and further with each passing day, was dropping precipitously behind a beach umbrella. This sun, by the way, remains far the most important of life's neglected things, the first prerequisite of life, literature, and agriculture. I liked to think about the topography of that special star, the mountains, sunbeam horses feeding on sparks, ecstatic surfers riding to shore on waves of chartreuse glass.

"And that tousled-headed son of his!" (Incredibly, they were still speaking about the fat man.) "I expect that boy makes real good money teaching corporate people how to cheat on taxes."

"And his wife?"

"Feminist."

We watched him fade around the bend. He was as white as paper, but his feet were shrewdly encased in black leather dress shoes capable of defending him against beer can tabs, burning cigarettes, and biologic litter of various sorts. Came then a heroic-looking life guard, a stalwart fellow with well-developed abs and peckers and the like.

"A very Achilles!" K exclaimed. "But hasn't learnt yet how to wipe himself."

"I wouldn't impugn Achilles that way," Casper said. "He was very brave. And chose everlasting fame over mere longevity."

"Oh look, here comes a little boy with a bucket and a wee little shovel. Look at that face!" (We laughed.) "Son-of-a-bitch doesn't have the faintest guess what life has in store for him. By God, he's going to put some sand in that bucket and run and show his mother. And have more fun in five minutes than Howard has had in seventy years."

"Seventy-five," I amended.

Happier still was the dog chasing along behind. His face alone had been worth our expenses.

"Admit it, people like us have no business trying to have fun. Can't be done."

We gathered that night about the television and after experiencing a newscast delivered by a good-looking blond female woman with an impressive chest, we turned to a crime drama centered upon a white male culprit addicted to torturing small black babies. Even more instructive were the advertisements. We watched with fascination as two English-speaking ducks had gotten into a conflict over a brand of car wax. Came next a shapely woman in a bikini recommending a breakfast cereal. Anyone investing in that product stood a good chance of copulating with this girl. Just then a voice broke in. Zinc futures, down this morning, were coming back up!

We stayed for the presentation of a military award to a front-line female combatant who had slain three Muslims in a bayonet charge. Regressive as I am, my mind flashed back to when girls were . . . I had almost said "demure!" We do get tired of being laughed at, you understand.

There followed a panel discussion on foreign policy, a serious program mediated by experts from the Northeast holding certificates from some of the most reprehensible educational institutions in the world. The gravamen, as I understood it, was that all countries everywhere ought be more like . . .

Us.

Twenty-Eight

It was at this time, or slightly before or after that I began to bring my diary to its foreseeable conclusion. My penmanship had always been exceptionally poor, and it had come to the point where I myself couldn't decode entries more than two days old. As for the gizmo, despite all its merits, it hadn't the capacity to make voice recordings, and I had perforce to call upon Casper to put on paper what you see here. Anyway our vacation was coming to its end.

We paid the cashier (a pea-brained adolescent who needed a computer to make the calculation), and then turned northward onto Highway 47.

"Here we are," Earl attested suddenly, "back in this old car again!" His brains were in conspicuous decline.

The day was bright by New Jersey standards, but the traffic was as slow and as exasperating as always. A person could use a bicycle and arrive in New York two hours earlier than we were likely to do. On the other hand, the migrants were more numerous (and more pathetic) than of just three days earlier, and we were obliged more than once to pull over and distribute a few leftovers and small coins.

The Frasier was driving poorly and constantly wanted to divagate off into used car lots, flea markets, free-standing dentists' booths, abandoned warehouses, photographers with tripods, balloon merchants, oyster stalls, and other typical ingredients of the state's landscape. We knew that we were drawing near the world's richest city when two men of foreign provenance suddenly dashed out into the highway and, reaching through the open window, attempted in vain to remove Casper's wristwatch. K wanted to run them down. Gwen forbade it.

"You want to be put in the electric chair?"

"They don't use that anymore."

"Oh? You'd be surprised what they can do to people like us." She swerved suddenly, avoiding the corpse of a farm animal of some type. Larger than a cat but smaller than a cow, the creature had lost some twenty feet of intestines now seen dragging from the bumper of a little yellow sports car running on ahead.

We never stopped, not till we had crossed over into Beauregard County and had come to a combination cafeteria and electronic games arcade made to look like an old-fashioned log cabin with a stone chimney and cardboard chicken cutouts staked in the ground. The waitress, a tough-looking quantity with a Brooklyn accent, had been fitted with a bonnet and a corncob pipe. As to the menu, it offered buttermilk biscuits and sweet tea along with blintzes and gefilte fish. Us, we ordered coffee. There was some evidence that cigarettes were available—provided one could cite the secret word. Many tried, few succeeded. Our group mostly needed to visit the restroom, a collective endeavor where Earl was concerned. Upon K and myself devolved the privilege of conducting

him to the facility and holding him upright until at last he
managed to empty at least one sector of his chambered
bladder. That was when we observed a man peering at us
over the top of his stall. This was a real danger. We knew
well the penalties for rejecting scopophile advances.

"Can't help you," K responded. "We're in a hurry."

It's an uphill journey, as maps agree, when traveling
northward. We passed hurriedly through a down-and-out
sort of town populated mainly by a Hamitic people in
loose slacks. The car was behaving beautifully for its age,
and the stereo had this real mellow quality that sorted
perfectly with Mahler's autumn song in *Das Lied von der
Erde*. But soon we began to be overtaken by ambulances
and police cars, followed immediately by the first warning
of the eleven o'clock pollution release. That was when I
changed over to the Berlioz *Requiem*, and after draining
off a moiety of vodka, a small one, passed it up to Morgan.
New York was just ahead.

It was a good thing, arriving at my furnished apartment
before the rain. There was some material in my mailbox,
advertisements for the most part, including a free copy of
a magazine issued by a support group for endangered
meese. Or mooses probably they should have said. I was
asked to join a wine drinking society, to be the first to in-
vest in digital underwear, to reserve a subscription to a
gold-tooled edition of Stephen King, a pound of kudzu
seeds, a set of programmable dice, a twelve-pack of penile
extenders, and an American flag endorsed by a well-
known golfer. Of authentic mail there was but one single
letter from that same middle age man who for the past
twenty years had claimed, correctly, to be my cousin.

No one had penetrated my flat, as I could attest from
the knob left by me in the clock position of about 2:30
p.m. It was good to step inside my customized domain
and reacquaint myself with the two large and one small

rooms where my music and books, my ammunition, distilled water, and canned foods were organized in tidy array. I might be quarantined for life by the New York police, but still I could have sustained myself for a full five, possibly six days, depending on the drawdown of my water reserves.

All my lizards had absquatulated, but I was rather quickly able to find their hiding place and tempt them forth with the last of the frozen crickets. Dust, it is true, had carried out its unwelcome mission, requiring me to waste time transferring the stuff—it could not be destroyed—with a damp chamois cloth. Had someone entered my sanctuary by way perhaps of the window—I hadn't thought of that—and purloined some of my books and signed photographs? I was pretty certain she had not.

I slept that night beneath presumed myriads of bright spiny stars which could not however be viewed from my location. Thereafter I read for less than an hour in my long-neglected *Necronomicon*, a gift just two weeks before he murdered himself from one of my best all-time students. I blame myself for that tragedy, as for any other of my acolytes taught to see the country as it really is.

Twenty-Nine

The following days were unpleasant. The escrubilator was in Gwen's control, and though she had promised not to harm it, how could I be certain? More than that, it was past time to decide what to do with the world, now that social conditions were so much worse than of just a few weeks earlier. My neighbor had contracted the sixth in a series of hundred-day marriages, while his sensitive son had found a vacant loft in Greenwich Village. And although black and brown people were being discouraged from using the procedure, the government had appropriated generous funds to defray the high cost of sterilization of white women.

Thus ends the great Western Civilization, starting with the Myceneans and finishing, not with earthquakes and pandemic, but something rather more serious than that.

"What?" someone will ask. "What could be more serious than that? What could possibly be worse than all those earthquakes and so forth? Anyway, I don't believe you."

"Much worse."

"Oh, you just like to talk that way. Come on, admit it."

I admitted nothing. Knowing what was in store for the world, the more pressing question was whether it mightn't be better to end the species altogether. A new Permian Extinction, and a chance to strangle equality in its cradle! No more decadence, no more democracy and women who'd rather be men. An end to prosperity, and best of all no more cities under the sun! It was with these issues in mind that I called a meeting of us last good men for Friday the 21st, to take place in our special location.

Came the day. Or night rather. At first we simply exchanged pleasantries and shook hands all around. She had brought the escrubilator, had Gwen, and passed it over to me before anyone had actually gotten drunk. We discussed all sorts of things, which is to say until Casper spoke out loud and clear:

"But isn't it possible that the country still has *something* good in it? Something buried deep in the national subconscious?"

"Nope."

"Something that might yet awaken, like a bear when winter is done?"

"We've already discussed this! This 'something' you're always talking about was the product of a certain people at a certain time."

"He's right. We couldn't have set up the Chinese culture, nor they ours. Better to kill the whole world than let history's only good civilization go down the drain."

"God, you're a hard man!"

"Should have done it years ago. Before it had come to this." (This was K's view, indubitably the most militant, most bitter, and most dangerous of us all.)

"They killed a bunch of us in Philadelphia last night. Did you read about that? They couldn't produce enough money, and so they had their bellies slit open."

We drank. The inn had closed by now, wherefore the owner, a man not entirely opposed to our views, conducted us down into the second level basement stocked by us with a small collection of fundamental texts, one of them mine. No one could hear us and the beer was in good supply. Spoke then Earl:

"Could we really kill everybody in the whole wide world Howie? Honestly?"

"Well! Not all at one time certainly. Patience will be needed. And besides, once we've gotten rid of the worst ones . . . Who knows? Perhaps the others will change their ways."

"They still need to be punished. For what they did before they changed."

"God, you're a narrow-minded son-of-a-bitch. Tell me K, what exactly did you used to do before *you* changed?"

"I never changed. I have spent my whole time in search of transcendent values."

"He's telling the truth."

"And did you find any? Transcendent values?"

"You've heard him on the piano. Plays *transcendently*, if I may say so."

Bored with such elevated talk, the woman had taken out her glasses and her knitting and was inspecting a seam where two colors had run up against each other. Would I really be able—this is what I asked myself—willing and able to discontinue millions just like her? Mediocrities in spite of their efforts? I bethought me then of the final parts of the *Götterdämmerung,* wherein an entire civilization had been put aside to make place for something better. And then, too, there were times when I had advanced intuition of that improved world, a composite society with borrowings not just from Greece alone, but also Sumeria, Florence, the *Belle Époque,* Elizabethan London, not to mention the things that might be going on at just this moment in the remote regions of outer space. Followed then several minutes in full silence, till Earl said this:

"It's hard for me to realize that we're actually thinking about this."

"It's hard for all of us."

"I mean! It's their world Howie, not ours, and they have every right to be as awful as they wish."

"There is no such right! Than to be like one of these, better were it not to be."

"Alright, how about this—instead of killing people, we just kill ourselves? We don't belong here anyway."

"No reason we can't do both. Them first and then us."

"Yes, I like that. Me, I've only got a few months anyhow."

"What? What did you say just now?"

"No, it's quite true. I'll be in the ground before Christmas comes."

We looked at him. His health, always marginal, was revealed in his posture, his palsy, and the pale blue film shutting off the vision in his last usable eye. Earl spoke:

"Well if Casp is dying, I'm dying too by God!"

"I can't believe we're talking like this. Doesn't seem real somehow."

"Now just hold it right there! Earl can't die, not so long as he's got that woman living with him."

"Gwen? She'll come, too. Won't you dear?"

"Maybe so, but . . . Hey! Where's *he* going?"

The fifth man, called Morgan, had arisen and departed

in some haste. As the foremost man in the group, I felt I should be giving a better direction to the conversation. We were all old men, save only Gwen, who still had some good years, pretty good, at her disposal.

"I don't know. Just doesn't seem real."

"Doesn't seem real to have just one leg either! Or less than one eye. Besides, I got a whole big stack of unpaid bills."

"Bills? Your life wouldn't be any good even if you had money in the billions. Hasn't anyone ever bothered to explain this to you?"

Silence fell over the group. It is true that Casper's situation was and for a long time had been somewhat of a burden both on him and us. A candid person would have admitted that his stump and cloudy eye were unpleasant to look upon. And besides, he was three-fourths in the grave already and I no longer expected him to repay the few small debts he had incurred with Gwen and me.

"Excuse me Casp," I asked compassionately, "but when do you plan to carry it out? This thing we've been talking about?"

"Not today. And not tomorrow. No, I want to wait till we've slaughtered the people on Earl's list."

"The hedge fund people?"

"No, no, no. Those who opened up our borders."

We voted. By the tiniest of margins, the crippled man's choice was ultimately confirmed.

Thirty

It was past midnight four days later when K appeared at my door and pleaded for the gizmo. He wanted to do the deed himself (disaggregating evil people) and would absolutely not agree to bring about his own end without first accomplishing this one last benefit to civilization. We argued about it, although I could see the advantages of his

proposal. In spite of everything, in spite of my affection for
the mid-century America, in spite of passing the last several decades in a state of extreme depression, and in spite
of several other things as well, I at last gave in to him. Together we wrapped the device in canvas and bound it up
with cord. Anyone seeing it from a remove of, say, two
yards or more would have thought nothing of it. In fact,
no one would have thought much about it at any distance.

"You *will* end yourself, no?"

"You go first."

"Can't. We have a meeting scheduled for week after
next."

He laughed. No one would have described it as genu-
inely a cheerful laugh however. Much the contrary!

"Actually, I look forward to it. And you?"

"I plan to follow Casp."

"Casp? He took care of all that two days ago."

"Blimey! How'd he do it? No, don't tell me."

"Alright."

"Didn't use a gun did he?"

"Of course not. Ole Casp was far too ingenious for that.
The coroner couldn't believe it."

We shook again. Did I regret bidding farewell to a
mechanism that had absorbed a quarter of my working
life? Little bit. Was I excited by the prospect of a "surgical," as some call it, a surgical demonstration of what
should occur to evil people? I allow one guess only, and
now the time is up.

Thirty-One

Howard's last days! First he composed a testament
granting the gizmo and half his cumulated $366,200 to an
assassination cell organized by old white males. Next he
went to what probably would be the last performance of a
certain opera deemed too elitist for the new America. My

books I gave to young Christopher Martin, a socio-crystallographer living with a brunette in southeastern *Tierra del Fuego*. Of my wardrobe, furniture, art prints, musical recordings, all this I destroyed lest it fall into the hands of mediocre people.

I was enjoying an excellent meal of ham hocks, black-eyed peas, and biscuits in my second-favorite restaurant when came the news over TV of the "disappearance" (granulation actually) of an important banker last seen *en route* to a highly crucial international conference having to do with factors related to naked options on currency exchanges. The cost of water purification equipment had reached crisis proportions, and meantime the auction price of treasury notes had for the first time caused interest rates to break the thirty percent barrier. What can I say? I hastened to the men's room and did all I could to contain my laughter, an unsuccessful effort that seemed to perturb the man in the neighboring stall. Embarrassed, I returned to my lonely little table where I still continued to attract more attention than I wanted. "Disappeared," they said. Ah, K, K, K, what *have* you done?

Thirty-Two

I had two urgent and five semi-important tasks awaiting me before exiting post-modernity, namely providing for my lizards, finishing the remains of my Ecuadorean rum, and those five other things. To begin, I poured a strong measure of liquor into a measuring cup and mixed it with the small remains of my store of distilled water. Semi-inebriated, I started to kiss my pets goodbye, but then leapt back in horror when I took a close look, closer than before, at their ghastly faces. My intention was to post the creatures off to Chris Martin now lodged in a small town in southernmost Argentina.

I won't know the exact moment of my own "disappear-

ance." It's just past ten in the morning, too late to go back
to that aforementioned grimoire that had afforded me
some very peculiar reading these past days. Nor did I wish
to crank up *Parsifal* at this hour, lest I get into an emotional state. Instead I switched on the television and
mixed another drink. Stock prices were doing just splen-
didly, despite nagging doubts about the country's trade
balance. It had gone up and down, that balance, for hundreds of years, but matters were rather more serious now.
Corn futures were in play. Yes, and what had the Greeks
been doing at this stage in their own national decay? Or to
put it in Roman terms, it must be about 450 AD by now.
Continuing forward, the television blond revealed that
Caucasian peoples were now under thirty-two percent in
seven of the states with current trends portending even
further progress.

But we still had a way to go. My federal representative
had just celebrated the anniversary of his marriage to
three other males. A basketball player had renegotiated
his contract to $667,000 a week. Next, we were given an
interview with the man himself, a tall individual with a
primeval face. If Americans loved this sport more than
wife or children, who could be so churlish as to complain?
Came then an advertisement in which a hapless white
male was shown trying unsuccessfully to boil an egg. Next
the music, a tribal chant that harkened back nostalgically
to the glory that was pre-imperial Africa.

"Ah, me," I said. "And yet I feel quite certain that it
wasn't always this way." (I longed to die, and then to
awaken in a distant universe in which the population is
small, every man has a fine library, a thousand acres of
rich bottomland, and about 200 slaves.)

My rum was mostly gone. I don't pretend to understand what Earl and his woman will be doing. I do have
full confidence however in K. How strange, that within an
hour I shall have stepped into a parallel universe, just as

soon as I will have finished my little diary, herewith almost accomplished now. But can we really be talking about this? I who had never wanted anything more than just *one perfect moment,* one only, and to abide with it forever.

ABOUT THE AUTHOR

Tito Perdue was born in 1938 in Chile, the son of an electrical engineer from Alabama. The family returned to Alabama in 1941, where Tito graduated from the Indian Springs School, a private academy near Birmingham, in 1956. He then attended Antioch College in Ohio for a year, before being expelled for cohabitating with a female student, Judy Clark. In 1957, they were married, and remain so today. He graduated from the University of Texas in 1961, and spent some time working in New York City, an experience which garnered him his life-long hatred of urban life. After holding positions at various university libraries, Tito has devoted himself full-time to writing since 1983.

His first novel, 1991's *Lee,* received favorable reviews in *The New York Times, The Los Angeles Reader*, and *The New England Review of Books*. In addition to the present volume, his novels include *The New Austerities* (1994), *Opportunities in Alabama Agriculture* (1994), *The Sweet-Scented Manuscript* (2004), *Fields of Asphodel* (2007), *The Node* (2011), *Morning Crafts* (2013), *Reuben* (2014), the *William's House* quartet (2016), *Cynosura* (2017), *Philip* (2017), *Though We Be Dead, Yet Our Day Will Come* (2018), *The Bent Pyramid* (2018), *The Philatelist* (2018), and *The Smut Book* (2018)—which have been praised in *Chronicles: A Magazine of American Culture, The Quarterly Review, The Occidental Observer*, and at *Counter-Currents*.

In 2015, he received the H. P. Lovecraft Prize for Literature.